YOU'VE GOT IT, BABY!

You've Got It, Baby! is a work of fiction. All references to persons, places or events are fictitious or used fictitiously.

You've Got It, Baby!
Copyright © 2017
Mike Carmichael

Cover concept and design by David Warren.

Published by WordCrafts Press
Cody, Wyoming 82414
www.wordcrafts.net

"a Love Comes to Winston novel"

You've
Got It, Baby!

MIKE CARMICHAEL

All of my best!

[signature]

WordCrafts

"A walk in the park...

The song of the lark...

You've got it, Baby!"

CHAPTER 1

Mick popped the gearshift into neutral and allowed the vintage 'Vette to drift to a lazy halt at the four-way stop. The top was down, the air was clear, the early summer sunshine was tinged with warmth, and the road was quiet. It was hard to not drift into a state of sheer bliss on such an idyllic Saturday morning. Even better, there was hardly any traffic on the rural two-lane road entering Winston to distract his attention.

Mick depressed the clutch, slapped it into first and fed the old Corvette some gas, He eased off the clutch, grinning as the side pipes issued a low, rumbling roar, like an angry giant rudely awakened. As he pulled into the intersection, he caught sight of a petite, redheaded woman in obvious distress, waving madly toward him, trying to attract his attention. She was clutching something tightly to her chest.

Against his better judgment, Mick pulled the car into the parking lot of Winston Faith Center and Academy where the woman was standing, and shut off the ignition. He pulled off his sunglasses and he stepped out of the car, careful to keep the car door between himself and the rapidly approaching woman. He relaxed his guard when he saw the woman's burden; a pale and unresponsive child.

"Need help," he asked.

"My b-baby. She's… My car won't start and I can't find my cell phone and no one will stop and help and…" The woman broke down, sobbing uncontrollably. Mick reached for the child, a little girl no older than three. She was hot and flush, barely conscious and straining to breathe. He didn't think twice.

"Come on. Let's get you to the hospital." He took the woman by the arm and led her to his car. Once she was settled in the passenger's seat, he handed her the child. There was car seat, but desperate times call for desperate measures, he reasoned. "Hold her tight, OK?"

He jumped behind the wheel, turned the key and jolted the classic sports car to life. A quick glancing over his shoulder to make sure the road was clear, and he raced onto the street. He made a rolling stop at the next intersection, downshifted and turned left. "The Interstate is up ahead and the hospital is maybe four miles." Mick flashed a quick glance at the woman, then turned his full attention to the road. Ending up in a ditch wasn't going to help anyone.

"How is she?"

"Hot…and dry," the woman sobbed.

"Just hold her. It's okay. We're close. Just a few more minutes. He downshifted to second and swerved right, the 'Vette clawed for purchase, its rear end fishtailing, then roared up the on-ramp onto the freeway.

The woman braced herself and her child as the force of the sports car's acceleration pressed her against the side. The engine's roar was deafening, and she wondered if the vehicle was even still on the ground. As they flew past the few cars that were on the road she prayed. What was in her heart was, *Dear Lord, please touch Morgan and heal her. And please get us to the hospital safely, in Jesus name, Amen.* What came out of her mouth sounded more like, "Oh God, oh God, oh God." But she was pretty sure God knew what she meant.

The 'Vette blew past a black-and-white, doing 85 without slowing. The highway patrol trooper flipped on the cruiser's lights, hit the siren and fell in behind the speeding roadster. Mick spared a look in the rearview mirror, but refused to pull over. Instead, he waved frantically, pointing to the woman and child in the seat next to him. The trooper expertly maneuvered his cruiser along side the 'Vette, and saw the distressed woman and child; the woman mouthing 'Hospital!' through the window. The trooper nodded, pulled in front of Mick and led him toward the Emergency Room.

The few cars that were on the road parted for the flashing lights and siren, and Mick kept the Corvette on the trooper's tail. The trooper must have radioed ahead, because to Mick's amazement, emergency personnel were waiting with a gurney at the entrance to the ER. They took the sick child from the woman and whisked her away with the woman in their wake.

He called after her, "Can I call someone for you?"

"My parents, please," she called back and shouted the number before disappearing behind the hospital doors.

When Mick turned around, the state trooper had his citation book out and was writing furiously. He did not look happy.

The trooper finally looked up and gave Mick a blank stare. "License and registration, please," he said in a hard, flat voice.

"I saw the woman in a parking lot, and she looked really scared, and the baby was sick and..."

"License. And registration. Please," The cop repeated.

Mick reached into his pocket, pulled out his wallet, removed his license and handed it to the trooper.

"Connecticut." The trooper shook his head. "What brings you to Colorado?"

"I'm on vacation," Mick replied.

"And the lady?" The trooper handed Mick his license back.

"Never saw her before in my life," Mick retorted. Truth be told, he was starting to get more than a bit angry. He was the good guy after all; the White Knight who had saved the day. Why was this cop giving him the third degree? "I saw her in a parking lot, and she looked like she needed help. The kid was barely breathing. I tried to get her to the hospital, okay? That's it. You want to give me a ticket, do it."

The trooper merely shrugged. "Every cop in town is looking for you. You know how many people reported you?"

"No sir."

A slight grin turned up the corners of the trooper's mouth. "Get your car out of the ambulance zone before I ticket you." Then he turned and walked back to his cruiser. Before he got in, the trooper turned back to Mick.

"Great car. '66?"

"Thanks. '67."

Mick pulled the 'Vette into the visitor's parking lot. Finding a spot in the corner, he put the top up and reached for his cell.

CHAPTER 2

Mick loosened his tie as he sipped the waiting room coffee. The room was empty except for him. He thought, *At least the sofa is comfortable.* His coffee had grown tepid by the time a middle-aged couple burst through the door with a deer in the headlights look on their faces.

"Our daughter and granddaughter are here," the man demanded of the nurse at the reception desk. "Mackenzie and Morgan Austen."

Mick had no doubt about the identity of the couple. Although grey touched her auburn hair, and her face wore a line or two about the eyes, this woman bore a striking resemblance to the one who had recently occupied the passenger's seat in his car. He grimaced as he took another swallow of cold coffee while watching the scene at the nurse's station play out.

"Yes sir. They are in the exam area. The doctor is with them now."

"Are they okay?"

"At this point all I can say is the doctor is seeing them. Please have a seat in the waiting room. We'll call you when we have more information."

Frustration rolled across the man's face, but he finally nodded and led the woman into waiting room. Mick tossed the paper cup into the trash can, stood and walked to meet the couple. He extended his hand toward the man.

"Mr. Austen, I presume? I'm Mick Lambert."

Confusion played across the older man's face for a moment before recognition snapped into place. "You're the one who called us." He gripped Mick's outstretched hand and gave it a vigorous shake. "You're the one who brought them here. Thank you. I'm John Austen. This is my wife, Darla."

Mick noted the strength in the older man's grip and the quiet dignity in his voice as he returned the shake, then he nodded in acknowledgment toward Darla.

"Have you heard anything? Anything at all?" Mrs. Austen implored him, choking back tears. "I knew Morgan hasn't been feeling well lately but…"

The tears that had welled up behind her eyes overflowed, and once they started there was no staunching their flow. Her husband pulled her to his chest, comforting her as best he could.

"Darla, all we can do now is pray; just pray."

The man sounds like he actually believes what he's saying, Mick thought. He didn't often talk about his faith with strangers, but Mick thought this might be a good time to make an exception.

"Sir, I've been praying since getting here."

"Thank you, son. Thank you," the older man replied in a voice so warm it left no doubt of his sincerity.

Mick's confession of prayer ushered in a sense of calm that had been missing since the Austens' arrival. Darla took a deep breath and blew it out, her tears finally starting to subside. Together they sat, talked, paced and drank the strong, bitter hospital coffee while they waited for some word from the doctor.

Mick has long since learned the secret of forging friendships was to listen more than he talked. For the next 45 minutes, he sipped his coffee and nodded as John and Darla opened up about their lives. Mackenzie, the diminutive redhead, was their daughter. She worked as an English teacher at Winston Faith Academy where John served as the pastor and Darla worked as the school administrator. The couple had another daughter, he also learned, who was married and lived in Dallas. She too was a teacher.

"Mom, Dad."

Mackenzie entered the waiting room and both parents rushed to her, surrounding her with hugs and questions.

Mackenzie drew in a deep breath, then slowly blew it out. "Morgan has diabetes."

"Diabetes? She's only two! How? That can't be right." Darla shook her head. She rose and started pacing again in an unsuccessful attempt to prevent a fresh flow of tears.

"They did blood tests," Mackenzie explained, a quiet calm settling over her. "Her blood sugar was high. That's why she has been so sick lately, why she was hot and dry, throwing up and going potty so much." She gave her parents a determined look. "The doctor said Morgan will be alright. And she will. But we are going to have to learn to adjust our lifestyle."

John rose and put his arms around his wife. He held her for a moment as the diagnosis sank in.

"Can we see her?"

"Yes, but she's asleep. They gave her a sedative." Mackenzie's calm exterior started to crack, revealing the scared mommy inside. "Dad, she was so scared. The I.V., the needles, all the machines whirring and beeping." She stifled a sniffle, and took control of her emotions. "They need to keep her awhile, you know, to determine insulin type and dosage, her diet, those sorts of things. I need someone to go home and get her pajamas, and her bear, and…"

She suddenly noticed Mick.

"You're still here?"

Mick flashed a smile at her. "I couldn't leave without knowing how she is. If you want, I can take you home to pack a hospital bag, then bring you right back. The baby's asleep and your parents can stay with her."

He smiled again, causing an unfamiliar flutter in Mackenzie's stomach. *Who is this guy?* She thought. *An angel? A knight in shining armor? A good Samaritan isn't supposed to look like he just stepped out of an Armani ad.*

"You've been very kind, but I still have to meet the tow truck for my car, and I couldn't impose…"

"No imposition. I would like to."

That smile again.

"I promise we'll take it at a more leisurely pace this time."

Mackenzie looked to her parents for support, but Mr. Austen just nodded. She made up her mind.

"Alright then. Morgan's in Room 5." She exchanged quick hugs with her parents. "I won't be long."

"Nice to have met you," Mick shook the older gentleman's hand again. "I wish it had been under better circumstances."

"Thank you, Mick. For everything. I hope we see you again, so we can thank you properly."

Mackenzie led the way out of the hospital room and into the parking lot, then Mick took the lead, guiding her to the classic Corvette. He opened the passenger door for her.

"Wow. Pretty car," she said. "Can't say I really noticed it before. It's so shiny!" She fastened her seat belt. *I didn't notice how attractive he was, either, she thought. Black hair, deep blue eyes, killer smile, dimples, impeccably dressed. He is gorgeous! Whoa, slow down girl. You have a daughter to raise.*

Mick eased the 'Vette onto the street, keeping a weather-eye out for cops. He didn't want to risk a second stop in one day. The silence stretched out until it became uncomfortable. Mick attempted some light conversation. "So, your folks tell me you are a teacher?"

"Yes, I've been teaching for four years."

Silence.

"Do you enjoy your work?"

"Oh, yes."

More silence.

This time Mackenzie made the attempt at small talk.

"So, what line of work are you in?"

"Mmm, I'm in banking and finance. I'm something of a bean counter." As if reading her mind, he added, "It's really very enjoyable work."

He flashed another of those disturbing, giddy-making smiles as he pulled up behind her car. The tow truck was already waiting when they arrived.

"Well, Mr. Lambert," Mackenzie held out her hand for a shake. "Thank you. You have been more than kind."

Mick took her hand in his, but said, "Mick. Please."

"Alright. Thank you, Mick." She smiled back at him. *Two can play at this game,* she thought.

"May I call you Mackenzie?"

"I think maybe Miss Austen might do for now," she replied, a playful grin creasing the corners of her mouth.

"Miss Austen it is," Mick replied. If he was disappointed, he didn't show it. He reached into the inside pocket of his jacket and pulled out a pen and business card. "I want you to promise me that if I can help you, that you will call me. I've taken a house in town for the summer. My local number is on the back." He slipped the pen back in his pocket and handed her the card.

"And do you always get what you want, Mick Lambert?"

This time Mick really was taken aback. It was not the response he had expected and it left him momentarily speechless.

"What are you anyway?" Mackenzie didn't give him an opportunity to regain his mental footing. "Are you a Good Samaritan; a knight in shining armor?" She looked around her, caressing the upholstery. "Knights are supposed to ride white chargers, and this is not white and it is definitely not a charger. What kind of car is this?"

She gave him one of *those* looks, then laughed at the expression on his face—something between raw befuddlement and little-boy charm. Then his face began to change. His eyes sparkled and he threw back his head and laughed, long and loud. She liked the warmth of it.

"No. No, it's not a Charger. You are sitting in a fully restored, vintage 1967 Corvette. A Charger is a Dodge and this fine vehicle, M'lady, was manufactured by Chevrolet."

Mackenzie put her hand to her mouth and laughed.

"What's so funny?"

Her green eyes sparkled. "At first I thought you said, Gringolet."

"Gringolet?" Mick repeated, a blank look washing over his face. "I don't get it."

"Sir Gawain's horse," Mackenzie laughed. "I mean, it would be appropriate. If you really were a knight."

Now that he was let in on the joke, Mick laughed too.

Mackenzie opened the door, and stepped out.

"Here, let me help you," Mick offered.

"No need. But thanks."

Mick looked around the parking lot where Mackenzie's car waited. It was then that it dawned on him; they were in the parking lot of John Austen's church. And tomorrow was Sunday.

"Will you be here in the morning, I mean with your daughter in the hospital?"

"I don't know yet," she pondered. "I'm supposed to sing during the service in the morning, but I have those classes with the diabetes educator, and I'm sure Morgan is going to be terrified when she wakes up. Just gonna play this one by ear for now. Thanks again, Mick." She turned and walked to her car.

CHAPTER 3

Mick changed into his jogging sweats and set off on a two and a half mile run. He had come here to rest and relax, to think, to commune with God. Well, he was thinking all right. He was thinking of a ninety-five pound, five-foot tall, green-eyed, redhead named Mackenzie Austen. And he couldn't get her out of his head.

She had a daughter, he pondered as he ran. *So she must have a husband, right? But why no wedding ring. And why wasn't he at the hospital? And why does she go by the last name of Austen?*

The questions kept time with his steps, and he pressed forward up the hill.

Could it be that she had a child out of wedlock? No. Don't go there. Mackenzie is the minister's daughter. She sings in the choir. She told me so herself. She's not the kind to... No. Don't go there!

Mick was blowing hard by the time he walked up the drive of his rented home away from home. *It's not the distance,* he rationalized, *it's the altitude.* He unlocked the door and tossed his keys into the bowl on the counter before plopping down in the recliner. He grabbed his cell and started to dial the hospital, but hit the off button before the first ring. "I can't call,' he muttered aloud. "I would just be intruding. They don't really know me from Adam."

He put the cell phone on its charging pad, forced himself out of the comfy recliner and made his way to the bathroom for a long, hot, steamy shower. Once he had sluiced away two and a half miles worth of sweat, he wrapped a thick, cushy robe around himself, and wandered into the kitchen where he prepared a simple tossed green salad. Mick grabbed his Bible, the salad bowl and a bottle of spring water and headed for the back deck.

He had come to the quaint little town of Winston, Colorado to rest, relax and think - and to get a little closer to God – and that's what he was going to do. He settled into the deck chair and took in the view. So peaceful. So beautiful. Pristine valleys, blue skies, white snow capped mountains in the distance.

Still, all Mick could see was a pair of green eyes.

CHAPTER 4

"I'll get the rolls out of the oven, if you'll set the table," Darla Austen said to Mackenzie as bustled about preparing the evening meal. Morgan was sedated and resting comfortably in the hospital. Mackenzie hated being away from her, even for a moment, but she knew there was nothing she could do, at least for the moment. A good, hot meal would do her good, then she could head back to sit with her little girl.

"That Mr. Lambert seems like such a nice man," Darla continued to chatter as she worked.

"I guess so," Mackenzie replied. "Did he tell you much about himself? All he told me is that he works in banking or finance."

"Only that he's from Connecticut and he came here for a vacation," Darla answered as she brushed melted butter on top of the rolls. "He said he plans to stay the summer. Which seems odd. I mean, bankers don't take the summer off, do they? Call your father please. It sure is quiet without Morgan here."

Mackenzie poured iced tea as her parents sat down. The little family joined hands and John offered a simple grace. "We've added Morgan to the church's prayer chain," John told them between mouthfuls of roast beef and mashed potatoes. "There will be prayers going up for her health all over town by now."

Mackenzie tried to eat, but mostly she just pushed her food around on the plate. *Worry makes a poor sauce,* she thought.

"Mom, why did Morgan develop diabetes?" she asked. "None of our family has diabetes, do they? I'm pretty sure no one on Jared's side had it either."

"There was my great-uncle Howard on my father's side," Darla began. "No, he had gout."

"Mackenzie, you will wear yourself out trying to figure out why. Sometimes things just happen," John interjected. "Right now we have a diagnosis, so we can move forward. The best thing we can do now is just to trust God. He uses desperate measures to become doors of blessing."

Mackenzie's eyes flashed green fire.

"How?" she demanded.

She took a sip of iced tea while she waited for an answer. John lowered his fork to his plate and studied his distraught daughter for a long moment. He had counseled countless families and individuals who had gone through a myriad of tragedies during his years in the ministry. But it was somehow different when the person asking 'how' was your own child.

"Well, Baby, I don't know how. But what I do know is that with God, all things are possible." He wiped the corner of his mouth with his napkin. "Sometimes all we can do is trust and believe that He cares about us."

"But this is Morgan! And she's so little. And afraid." A tear leaked from her eye and trickled down her face.

"Yes," John answered. "But God is so big and He fears nothing." He flashed her his most reassuring smile, the one that had chased monsters from under her bed when she was Morgan's age. Mackenzie have a quick, staccato laugh.

"Thanks Dad," she said. "I needed to hear that."

Darla reached over and patted her daughter's hand. "Baby, why don't you go back to the hospital and sit with Morgan. I suspect you'll rest better there in an uncomfortable hospital chair than you would in your own bed."

Mackenzie smiled, then stood. "Thanks mom. I don't know what I would do without you both. Here, let me help with the dishes first…"

"Go," Darla ordered. "Your father and I can take care of the dishes. You go take care of that baby."

Mackenzie nodded, then turned and walked out door.

CHAPTER 5

M ick wasn't sure what to expect when he walked through the doors of the sanctuary. He was accustomed to churches with an optimistic view of their congregation – half full. But even though it was still a few minutes before the start of the service, the room was already packed. He found a seat in the center section, sat, then looked around for the only three people there that he knew.

He was still looking when a screen lowered behind the pulpit. The musicians tuned up, the congregation quieted down, and there she was. Mackenzie, sporting a modest, light green dress, walked across the front of the platform, her curly red hair accenting her heart-shaped face.

Mick had come to worship God, but at the moment, his thoughts were distracted. *How beautiful she is*, floated through his mind, unbidden. He shook his head and tried to turn his focus back on the Lord.

Mackenzie picked up a microphone and raised it toward her mouth. Words to a praise song appeared on the screen behind her as she tilted her head back, closed her eyes and raised her voice. Mick had never heard anything like it.

This girl knew how to worship! She was an angel singing around the throne of God. Mick felt energy flow through him. It was like electric Jello!

Mackenzie led the congregation in several more songs of

praise and adoration, effortlessly ushering them into the presence of their Creator. She ended with a tender solo, replaced the microphone on its stand, then quietly walked off the platform and sat beside her mother.

John Austen took the pulpit. Rather than immediately launching into a sermon, he called for prayer requests from the congregation, offering time for personal ministry, and he shared about how Morgan was doing. It was obvious from the reactions that the little girl was a much beloved member of this flock.

Mick liked this church. *I'll be back*, he thought with an Arnold Schwarzenegger accent, and grinned to himself. Once the service ended, he made his way through the crowd down to where Mackenzie stood beside her mother, greeting other church members and guests.

"Well, hello Sir Mick," she smiled and extended her hand.

"Good morning. You sing like an angel!" He immediately regretted the over-the-top compliment, and felt more like a shy schoolboy with his first crush than a mature, successful businessman.

Mackenzie's cheeks flushed and she lowered her eyes. "Thank you," she giggled. Then she looked into his eyes. "Thank you for the balloons and the bear you sent to Morgan last night. She was thrilled. And it was so cute how you signed the card: *Gringolet.*"

Mick liked the sound of her laugh. He took his right fist, brought it over his chest, and lightly bowed his head.

"Oh, I am impressed. You are steeped in chivalry and knighthood." She graced him with a big smile.

"If it pleases, M'lady," he replied.

The crowd had thinned out and John approached from his place by the entrance where he had been greeting members of his flock. He put an affectionate arm around his wife's waist. "Glad you could make it, Mick."

"My pleasure. Great church. It's warm and friendly. Great worship. Oh, and it was a great sermon, too."

Together the foursome made their way out of the sanctuary and into the parking lot, talking as they walked.

"Nice save," John smirked. There was no doubt in his mind about the part of the service Mick most enjoyed. "Would you care to join us for lunch? Darla is a great cook."

"I don't want to intrude, and I know Mackenzie has to get to the hospital."

"It isn't an intrusion, Mick," Mackenzie insisted. "I have to get lunch and change before heading to the hospital. Please come."

"Come on," Mrs. Austen patted his arm.

"Wow, three against one. Okay, I'll come. If you're sure I'm not…"

A sharp look from Mackenzie cut him off.

"Okay, okay," he laughed. "I'll come. Mackenzie, would you care to ride with me?"

"Mmm, in Gringolet? Sure."

"Uh, I didn't bring Gringolet, uh, I mean, the Corvette."

"No Gringolet? What did you bring?"

"This." He pointed to a silver Mercedes Sedan.

Mackenzie tried not to look too impressed.

"I see. And just how many cars did you bring with you on your…vacation?"

Mick opened the passenger door and she stepped in.

"Two," he replied as he closed her door. He trotted to his side and hopped behind the wheel.

"Gringolet's my baby. I pamper her, but she's a classic. She's really not an everyday kind of car."

"Oh, Okay. So, how did you get two cars here from Connecticut?" Her head cocked to one side in curiosity. The Mercedes slipped effortlessly onto the street behind the Austen's SUV.

"I drove this and had the 'Vette shipped."

"That must have been terribly expensive," she said, then immediately regretted it. *That was rude,* she thought. *But if he can afford a Mercedes and a classic car, he must be...* her thoughts ground to a halt at the obvious conclusion.

Mick just smiled and they drove the rest of the way to the Austens' ranch-style home in silence.

Mick parked and helped Mackenzie out. Darla called out, "I hope you like lasagna, Mick."

"Sure do," Mick called back."

Mackenzie led him down the walkway and through the front door. She pointed to the guest bathroom. "You can wash up in here. Mom has everything all ready. We just have to pop it into the oven to get it good and hot."

The house was warm and cozy, like a real home. Mick liked it.

As they sat around the table, John extended his hands. "Hope you don't mind, Mick. We always join hands when we give thanks."

Mick took Darla's hand on his left and Mackenzie's on his right. He couldn't help noticing how small and warm good it felt, holding it... *Stop it! You're supposed to be praying,* he thought.

Mackenzie felt her heart was pounding inside her chest. She bit her lip and hoped Mick wouldn't notice. *Lord, why do I feel like a schoolgirl all of a sudden?*

Then John started to pray. Mick thought it sounded more like a man talking to a dear friend than the formal prayers he was used to.

"Lord, thank you. You have given us so much, and we are

grateful. Bless our meal and our time together. And Lord, be with little Morgan. You know how much we lover her, and we know how much You love her. Heal her Lord. Oh, and thanks for sending Mick to our table, Lord. I think he may be a keeper. In Jesus name. Amen."

As the food was passed from hand to hand the conversation took on a light, familial tone, most of it centering around Morgan, but there was also plenty of good-natured teasing and laughter around the table. It felt good to Mick, like sitting down to dinner with some old friends.

At last Mick made a decision. He cleared his throat. "I should probably tell you a bit about myself," he began. "When I came to Winston, I didn't really expect to form any relationships, so it never occurred to me to tell anyone who I am."

Mick's confession was met by blank stares. He pressed forward.

"It was never my intention to deceive anyone. It just didn't seem to be all that important before. But since I'm going to attend your church for the foreseeable future, I thought, well, maybe you should know."

Blank stares morphed into curious looks, but no one else around the table said a word.

"Well, for starters, my name is Mick Lambert. My full name is Michael David Lambert, IV. My grandfather called me 'Mick,' and it just stuck."

"Oh my," Darla exclaimed.

If John was surprised, it didn't register on his face. He simply nodded and took another sip of iced tea.

"I thought you looked familiar," he said. "Of course I've read about you in the newspapers. Didn't expect to have you sitting at my dinner table though."

Mackenzie glanced from her mother's face to her father's in

complete bewilderment. Finally, she turned her attention to Mick. "I'm afraid I don't understand."

"Um, have you heard of The Lambert Group? Lambert Financial? Lambert Industries? Lambert Construction? I could go on," Mick said with a sheepish look on his face.

Mackenzie's eyebrows rose as realization flooded her face. "Oh. You're one of *those* Lamberts?"

Laughter tickled the corners of Mick's mouth as he replied, "Well, I suppose that depends on how you feel about *those* Lamberts."

"So what brings you to Winston?" John asked.

"Grandfather died six months ago and left me the company, lock, stock and two smoking barrels, as the saying goes. The transition was pretty intense, and once it was completed, well, honestly, I just wanted to get away for a while."

"According to the article I read in *Inc. Magazine*, you were raised by your grandfather, right?"

"Yes sir. My parents both died in a plane crash when I was roughly Morgan's age, and my grandmother passed away when I was four. The only family I ever knew was Michael David Lambert, Jr."

"So you run Lambert Group?" Mackenzie's bewilderment had shifted into full-blown fascinated now.

"Yep. My business card says, 'CEO.' It's mine. I own it. Now, I don't really run the day to day operations. I make the final decisions, and have final approval authority…I'm sorry, I'm going on and on. I didn't mean to bore you with the nit-picky little details."

Darla squeezed his hand. "You've done nothing worthy of an apology."

"Well, you certainly pricked my curiosity," Mackenzie

confesses. "Why did your grandfather call you Mick?"

Mick grinned. "When I was little, I was a huge Mickey Mouse nerd. Still am."

"Sounds like you miss him."

"Yeah, he was quite a guy."

"Your grandfather was a heckuva businessman," John said, "but he also had quite a reputation for being honest and fair; a real Christian."

"Yes sir. He raised me in church. He was a tough negotiator and drove a hard bargain, but nobody could say anything bad about his character."

Mackenzie looked at her watch. "Visiting hours start soon. I need to get changed Will you excuse me?" She pushed her chair back and stood.

"Um, Mackenzie? If it's alright with you, may I come to visit Morgan with you? I mean, I know you barely know me, and I don't want to get in the way or anything, but…"

Mackenzie smiled at him and cocked her head in a most fetching manner. "Well of course you may. I'm sure Morgan would love to meet her knight; even though she won't get to meet Gringolet," she laughed. "Let me change and I'll be right back."

John and Darla exchanged confused glances. "Gringolet?"

"It's a long story," Mick said with a wry smile.

CHAPTER 6

Mackenzie changed into jeans and sneakers with a knit pink short-sleeved top, and tied her hair back in a loose ponytail held in place with a pink scrunchie.

Mick held the door for her as she hopped into the front seat, then trotted around to the driver's side and climbed in beside her. *She looks great!* The thought popped into his head unbidden, and he found himself having unaccustomed trouble keeping his eyes on the road and off of his traveling companion.

"So, where did you learn to sing so well," he asked in an awkward attempt at making small talk.

Mackenzie shrugged. "I don't know. Singing is just something I've always done. I never really took any lessons. I guess I've just got the music in me," she giggled.

Mick was enchanted by the sound of her voice, the timber of her laughter.

"Singing just makes life, I don't know, better," Mackenzie continued. "I sing when I'm happy, I sing when I'm sad, and sometimes I even sing when I'm angry. It just helps, you know? Then when Morgan came along I found a whole new reason to sing." She giggled again as a sudden thought flitted through her mind. "You'll probably think this is funny, but when Morgan was still a tiny little baby I used to sing her to sleep with 'I've Got a Crush on You.'"

"The old Sinatra song? Sweetie Pie?"

"Uh-huh," Mackenzie laughed out loud at the memory. "It always worked like a charm. Morgan still asks me to sing it to her sometimes, when it's late and she is really sleepy. Do you sing?"

Mick gave her a sidelong glance as he turned into the hospital parking lot. "Oh, no. I'm afraid my musical ability consists of turning on the radio, and even then I get static half the time." He parked the car and jumped out to open her door. Mackenzie already had it opened and was standing outside the car before he could display his gallantry.

"Hey, give a guy a break," he gave a mock whine. "I'm trying to be a gentleman here."

"Sorry," Mackenzie countered. "I guess I'm just used to doing for myself. Besides, I am in a bit of a hurry. I'm supposed to have a meeting with the educator and I don't want to be late. I'm still processing this whole diabetes thing. I just want to make sure I do everything right. There's just so much to learn and I don't want to hurt Morgan because of something I don't know."

"You won't," Mick encouraged her with a smile as they entered the hospital lobby. "They'll teach you what you need to know. You'll be fine, you'll see. Morgan will be out and about in no time."

Butterflies started playing tackle football in Mackenzie's stomach when she saw his smile. She forced herself to look away. Stop it! You're not a school girl. "You're probably right," she replied as they rode the elevator to the pediatrics ward on ninth floor.

The elevator doors opened into hallways painted in bright pastel colors with cartoon characters dancing along the walls. The sounds of children either crying and laughing, wafted down the halls. Mick followed Mackenzie, who appeared to know exactly where she was going. They stopped half way down the hall at the nurses' station.

"Hello Ms. Austen. How are you today," the duty nurse asked. She handed Mackenzie an envelope. "The D.E. left this for you."

Mackenzie opened the envelope and pulled out several pamphlets along with a short note. A slight frown creased her lips. "Well, it seems I'll have to wait till tomorrow morning to meet with the diabetes educator," she sighed. She turned back to the nurse. "Is Morgan in her room or the playroom?"

"The playroom. Oh, and Dr. Brock should be coming around anytime now, so it's probably a good time for Morgan to return to her room."

"Okay," Mackenzie replied, her customary good humor returning. "This is Mick Lambert, a friend of the family. He has my permission to visit Morgan." She waved at the nurse and walked off with Mick following behind.

"Playroom," Mick asked as he caught up to her.

"Mmm hmm. Kids get bored quickly just lying in a hospital bed all day. Unless they're contagious, they let them play together. I just makes life easier for everyone involved. Right over there," Mackenzie pointed to a set of double doors at the end of the hall.

The room was laid out like a day care nursery, with thick mats on the floor, toys, child-sized tables and chairs with crayons and coloring sheets, puzzles and stuffed animal, and six toddlers contentedly playing-ring-around-the-rosie. A nurse smiled as they walked in.

"Morgan! Hi! Come here, Baby." Mackenzie bent down arms outreached.

"Mommy, Mommy." Morgan released the hands of her

new-found friends and abandoned the rosie-ring as she ran to Mackenzie and threw her arms around her neck. Mackenzie hugged her, picking her up.

"How are you feeling, Baby? Better?"

The little girl gave her a big grin and nodded her head.

Smaller than I remember, Mick thought as he watched the scene unfold. *Boy, she sure looks like her Mama; that same curly red hair, same green eyes and heart-shaped face, same mischievous smile.*

"Morgan, I want you to meet Mick. He helped us the other day when you were so sick and he sent you the balloons and the teddy bear. Can you tell him, 'Hello,' and 'Thank you?'"

Morgan cocked her head the same way Mick had seen her mother do and smiled.

"Hello and t'ank you," the child said is a soft but confident little voice. The she held up her arm to show off her hospital identification bracelet. "I gotta pretty bracelet, see?"

Mick admired the circle of plastic.

"You sure do, and it is certainly very pretty," Mick replied. "And you are welcome."

Morgan laid her head on her mother's shoulder as Mackenzie carried her back to her room, but her eyes didn't leave Mick's face.

Mackenzie started to set the child in her bed, but Morgan fidgeted and declared, "Potty, Mommy."

Mick sat on a comfy chair by the window while Mackenzie took Morgan to the bathroom. A few minutes later they reentered the room, and Morgan immediately walked over and climbed into the chair beside Mick.

"She doesn't wear diapers," Mick asked. "I'm no expert on early childhood development, but she seems awfully young."

Mackenzie leaned back against the door laughed. "No, she doesn't wear diapers, but I don't take any credit for it. One day she just decided she was a big girl and was not going to wear them anymore. She still has an accident from time to time, but they're few and far between."

"I see," Mick said, then turning to Morgan, he asked, "How old are you?"

The child held up two fingers.

"Two and a half, actually," Mackenzie said.

A crisp knock on the door preceded a short, round-faced doctor with a receding hairline and a bad combover, followed by a young nurse.

"Hi, Morgan, how are you today?" He smiled at the child then turned his attention to Mackenzie, "Ms. Austen."

"Hi, Dr. Brock. This is Mick Lambert, a friend of the family."

Mick nodded to the doctor, then stood and said, "I'll wait in the waiting area."

The pediatric waiting room was smaller than its counterpart in the ER, but was more colorful. Mick stood at the window and studied the view below. He came to this quiet community to seek some solitude, pray and maybe find some answers. So far the solitude thing hadn't exactly worked out the way he had planned. A smile crept across his face as a pair of green eyes appeared in his memory. *Not that I'm complaining,* he thought. *Oh, well, it's not like I'm in some big hurry. So far, I've met some great people, found a church I actually feel comfortable worshiping in, and then there is Mackenzie. And that little Morgan is a heart-stealer. No, there really is no hurry at all.*

He had downed a cup of vending machine coffee, read a pamphlet on measles, flipped through a children's book he remembered from his childhood and was back looking out the window again when Mackenzie came in carrying Morgan, who did not look happy.

He gave them a big smile. "Everything alright?"

"Dr. Brock said she's doing well, but they want to keep her for a few days," she sighed. "With kids Morgan's age, insulin regulation is tricky. They grow so fast. I know I shouldn't worry, but I can't help it. There's just still so much that I don't know. I'll feel better after taking those classes. Thank God school is out."

Morgan wriggled until Mackenzie put her down, then the toddler ran to Mick and raised her arms, with full expectation that he would pick her up. Mackenzie's eyebrows raised.

"She has never taken to anyone quite so fast before," she said.

Mick scooped the child up and held her in his arms. She lifted a bandaged finger and held it in front of his face for his examination.

"That lady stick my finger," she said, revealing the source of her unhappiness.

Mick studied the finger for a moment, and then smiled, winked at Mackenzie and gave the boo-boo a quick kiss.

"Were you a brave girl?" He set the child down, pursed his lips and brought both arms around her until his palms were two inches apart. "Were you this brave?" His voice was a cartoonish falsetto. He widened the gap between his palms to two feet. "Were you this brave?" His voice grew deeper. Finally, he threw his arms opend wide and in a deep, resonate baritone he says, "Or were you this brave."

Morgan shrieked in laughter, throwing her little head back and clapping her hands. She threw her arms as open wide as she could to indicate how very brave she had been.

Mick took her hand gently and studied the finger where

it had been stuck. Leaning forward again, he brought his left hand in front of Morgan. He took his index finger and thumb almost together and in a squeaky little voice said, "I bet that didn't hurt this much!"

Morgan thought that to be the funniest thing she had ever seen, and howled in laughter. Mackenzie took it all in. She found herself, inexplicably on the verge of tears. She had known the security and joy of having a loving father; her little girl had never known that relationship and it pricked her heart.

The door to the waiting room opened and the Austens came in, followed by a man, woman and little boy. The woman strongly resembled Mackenzie and her mother.

Mackenzie sprang to her feet and threw her arms around her. "Wendy, you came! I am so glad to see you." She turned to the sandy-haired man next to her and drew him into a familiar embrace. "Bryan, thank you for coming." Next she turned to the boy, who looked to be around six years old. "Adam, come and give me a hug," she commanded in loving voice. She drew the boy to her and gave him a big, wet kiss on the cheek, which he quickly rubbed off.

"One of these days you might discover you like kisses from girls," John Austen laughed.

Wendy crossed to Morgan, arms outstretched.

"Hey, Baby, come see Aunt Wendy!"

The toddler considered the request for a moment, cocked her head in a childlike imitation of her mother, then ran into her arms. Wendy gave Morgan a big hug, then shot a questioning look at Mackenzie.

Mackenzie returned the look with a quizzical grin that looked very much like a cat who had just eaten a canary. "Everyone, I want you to meet Mick Lambert," she announced. "Mick, this is my sister Wendy Collins; her husband Bryan and my nephew Adam."

Mick nodded at Wendy, then reached out to shake hands with Bryan.

Mackenzie and Wendy shared surreptitious sisterly question-and-answer looks back and forth, then Mackenzie asked aloud. "How long can you stay?"

"We have to be back in Dallas by Tuesday night," Bryan answered. "We have a teachers' conference that starts Wednesday morning."

Darla Austen put her hand on Mick's arm. "They both teach at U. T. Arlington," she explained.

"It was great to meet you all, but I don't want to spoil the family reunion. Mackenzie, I know I drove you, I assume you can catch a ride home with your folks?"

"Yes, of course."

"Bye everyone," Mick said. He patted Morgan's hand and started for the door when the child suddenly threw her arms toward Mick and started wailing.

"Morgan, what on earth…" Mackenzie crossed to her sister and took Morgan in her arms. Morgan's cries calmed to a dull sniffle, but she still held out her arms toward Mick. Mackenzie looked over at him with a look of complete bewilderment on her face.

Mick came back and patted Morgan's back. "If it's okay with your Mommy, I'll come by and see you tomorrow, okay?" he whispered, looking up into Mackenzie's eyes for approval. Morgan sniffed and sobbed, but nodded her head.

Mackenzie could hardly think. He was so close she could smell his aftershave. "That… that would be fine," she managed to mumble.

Mick started back for the door, swallowing a nervous lump that had appeared in his throat. Everyone in the family watched him depart with bemused eyes, before turning their gaze back on Mackenzie.

"What?' she demanded, but the only answer she got was a soft chuckle from her father and a knowing glance from her sister.

CHAPTER 7

Mick's mind was a jumble of conflicting thoughts all the way home. He changed into sweats and went for a jog in an unsuccessful attempt to clear his mind. Five miles later a giggling little girl and her red-haired mama were still playing hopscotch with his thoughts. The only difference was now he was dripping with perspiration.

He walked at a more leisurely pace to allow his heartrate to return to normal before mounting the steps to his front door. Once inside he grabbed a bottle of room temperature water from the kitchen counter and guzzled it down in one long draught. He tossed the empty plastic bottle into the recycling bin, then started stripping off his sweats. A few moments later he was letting the pulsing stream of hot water from the shower wash away the sweat and leech the ache from his muscles.

Refreshed, Mick snagged another bottle of water from the counter, picked up the novel that was lying on his end table and strolled out onto the back deck to relax and catch up on his reading. The sun was just beginning to touch the horizon and God was busy painting the sky in colors he couldn't put a name to. It was all so peaceful and beautiful that he thought if he looked at it too long by himself, his heart would surely burst. This was beauty that was meant to be shared, not hoarded.

"God, are you trying to tell me something," he mused aloud.

"If You are, I'd appreciate it if You'd be just a little more clear."

Mick cocked his head, as if listening hard, but the only sound was a distant cicada. He shook his head and laughed at the notion that God might actually want to talk to him. He settled down on the wicker deck settee, propping a pillow behind his head for support and opened his book, when his cell phone rang.

"Hello?"

"Hello, Mick?" came a soft feminine reply.

"Mackenzie?"

"Yes, I'm sorry to trouble you."

"It's no trouble. What's up?"

"Well…um…it's just that…

"Mackenzie, what can I do for you?"

"I was wondering…I mean, I have to take that diabetes class tomorrow and I thought…" she took a deep breath, "Hoo boy, this is harder than I thought it would be. Morgan wanted me to ask if you would come and sit with her."

Mick was silent a moment.

"Morgan wants me to sit with her?"

"Yes."

Another awkward momentary silence.

"And what do you want?"

Now it was Mackenzie's turn to remain silent.

"I…would like for you to sit with her, too. I mean, if you're not busy with your business stuff and all. It shouldn't take too long. I've just got to sit through these classes for the next couple of days, then I can take Morgan home. Wendy is going to sit with her tomorrow, but then they have to fly back to Texas, and…well…"

"You have known me for all of two days," Mick interrupted

her. "Why do you trust me? For all you know everything I told you at lunch is a pack of lies."

"Oh, but it isn't."

Mick's eyebrows lifted. "How do you know?"

"I ran a background check on you. Winston's Chief of Police is an elder at our church. Dad called him."

Now his eyebrows climbed all the way into his hairline.

"You ran a background check on me?"

"I'm sorry. Are you mad? It seemed the prudent thing to do, I mean, under the circumstances. You have the right to be mad. I'm sorry. Never mind. I shouldn't have called."

"No. Wait," he laughed. "You absolutely did the right thing. I would have done the same thing if I were in your shoes."

Mackenzie let out a relieved giggle. "In fact, I'm holding your file in my hands right now, and it is very interesting."

"My file? What file?"

"Let's see; MBA Harvard, 30 years old, joined Lambert Group six years ago in the finance department and worked your way up through the ranks; oh my, two moving violations in the past three years!"

"Uh, does it list my credit score?"

More laughter. "No, it does not give your financial information, other than to note that you are quite wealthy and are a solid citizen. According to the chief's handwritten note on this report, and I quote, 'He doesn't need credit; he has more money than he knows what to do with.'"

Mick laughed. "I would be honored to sit with Morgan Tuesday morning, but I do have one condition."

"And what might that condition be?"

"Have dinner with me."

Mackenzie's heart skipped a beat, then started racing in

an attempt to catch up. "You want to have dinner with me?" she stammered.

"Yes."

There was that awkward silence again.

"Alright," Mackenzie finally managed. "But please, can we go someplace casual? Maybe some place where Levi's are the dress code? Do you even own any jeans?"

"Of course," Mick smiled. "You name the place."

"The Beef Rack."

"The Beef Rack?"

"Uh-huh. Delicious food, family dining, jeans and t-shirt kind of place."

"The Beef Rack it is. It's a date. Tomorrow night? 7:30?"

"Yes, Oh just one more thing."

"What's that?"

"Please leave Gringolet home. We don't want to wake up the neighbors," she laughed.

"You got it, Baby. Gringolet stays here."

"So... I'll see you then?"

"Yeah, I'll see you then."

"And Mick, thank you so much. You have no idea how much this means to me. I mean, to Morgan." Mackenzie could feel the heat rising in her face.

"Tell Morgan, I'm happy to be of service," Mick replied. If he noticed her fumble, he didn't let on. "Besides, what would Sir Gawain do?"

"Sir Gawain would probably bring Gringolet," she laughed. "Goodnight, Mick."

"Goodnight, Mackenzie."

Mick hung up the phone, allowing the sound of Mackenzie's name on his lips to resonate in his mind. He picked up the novel, opened it, then put it down again. The sun was now below the horizon, red streaks illuminated the mountain peaks, and an unaccustomed warmth flowed through his chest.

"So, God," he murmured quietly into the evening sky, "was that You?"

CHAPTER 8

Mackenzie was waiting on the porch when Mick turned into the drive the following evening. She did not wait for him to open her door.

"Good evening," she said clicking her seat belt.

"You make it hard for a guy to act like a gentleman, you know that?" he quipped as he slipped the gear selector into reverse and backed onto the street.

"A *real* gentleman doesn't need my help to *act* like a gentleman," she laughed. "So, you *do* own jeans." She studied his dark green, long-sleeved shirt with an embroidered image of Mickey Mouse peeking out of the breast pocket. "And that shirt. Oh, I love it!".

"I told you I like Mickey Mouse," he chuckled.

They made small talk while driving through the neighborhood, but as he merged into traffic on the highway, Mick cleared his throat. "I'm curious," he started. "Forgive me, I know it's none of my business, but where is Morgan's father?"

Mackenzie tensed up, balling her fist in her lap, then she took a deep breath and expelled it. The silence between them was palpable. "I'm sorry," Mick mumbled. "Like I said, it's none of my business."

Mackenzie shook her head. "No. It's okay. I just… I just never talk about him."

Mick nodded and allowed the silence to return. He passed

a police car that was parked just beyond a copse of trees, and checked his speed. He was going a couple of miles over the speed limit, but it appeared the cop was in a lenient mood. Mick backed off the accelerator anyway.

"I was a junior at the University of Colorado in Boulder when I met Jared." Mick cut his eyes briefly toward Mackenzie. Her eyes were straight forward, and focused on the road ahead. "He was young lawyer at the most prestigious law firm in town. I fell head over heels in love with him. We had a whirlwind courtship and got married as soon as I graduated. We had a fairy tale life: I started teaching school, Jared was a rising star at the firm and making a name for himself. We had friends, a luxury apartment, the whole nine yards."

Mackenzie swallowed and looked out the window, hesitating as the memories washed over her. "Then I got pregnant and everything changed."

Her voice turned flat, unemotional. "Jared said, 'We're too young to have children. We have our careers to think of. I don't want a baby. At least not now.' So I asked him, 'What was I to do? Tell her to wait for a more convenient time?' and he said, 'Yes. Just get rid of it. We can always have another later, when things are...'" Mackenzie stifled a sob.

Mick, gripped the steering wheel with both hands. He had no idea what to say that would make the situation less uncomfortable. But Mackenzie didn't even seem to realize he was in the car next to her. She was lost in the memory.

"'It.' That man called his own child, 'it.' He wanted our baby, my baby, to come at a more convenient time," she repeated. "He wanted me to just get rid of it. He wanted me to..." Angry tears welled up in Mackenzie's eyes and leaked down her cheeks.

"That was the moment when I stopped loving him. There was no way I was going to let some butcher… I would not give up my child. Not my child!"

Mick reached over and took her hand. "It's alright. No one is asking you to give up your child, Mackenzie."

"He did," she seethed, then silence reigned once more. It took a few moments, but Mackenzie regained control of her emotions and her memories. "I'm so sorry, Mick. Please forgive me."

"It's okay," Mick said. "I'm the one who asked."

"I moved out the next day. I couldn't live with him any more; not after he suggested…well, you know. I moved back home with my parents and started working at the Academy. Jared's National Guard unit got called to active duty and he shipped out to Iraq, where he was killed in action," she said, her voice flat, emotionless. "My husband, the war hero. How's that for irony?

"Morgan was born two months later. He never saw her, but then he didn't want her, so I don't suppose that was any great loss. I took my maiden name back. I didn't want Morgan to bear the name of a man who did not want her."

Mick shot a quick look toward Mackenzie, and she caught his eye. "Yes, Mick," she confessed. "I'm obviously still bitter about the whole situation. Believe me, I pray every night, begging God to help me forgive him, but it's just so hard!"

Mick looked straight ahead, studying the road. "I won't say I understand, because I don't. I don't understand how a man could not want his own child. And I don't understand how a man could ever let you go."

Another awkward silence settled over the car. Mick bit the inside of his cheek, trying to figure out how he managed to let that last sentence blurt out of his mouth. Mackenzie stared at his profile as he turned into the parking lot, wondering exactly what he meant by that.

Mick pulled into a parking space, dropped the gear shift into Park, and turned off the ignition key. He turned and faced Mackenzie and smiled. "Well, this has been…interesting. I will keep you and Morgan in my prayers. But now, we've got some serious ribs to consume. How 'bout we talk about something nice and safe, like the weather or nuclear disarmament?"

He flashed that smile again and Mackenzie thought her heart would melt.

CHAPTER 9

Mick took in his surroundings. The Beef Rack was the definition of rustic charm with its country red-checkered table-cloths and candles in mason jars on the tables. It was a far cry from the elegant restaurants his clients insisted on back home. He liked it. And he liked the company he was in. He looked straight into Mackenzie's eyes and smiled.

Lord in heaven, does he have to keep doing that, Mackenzie thought. She studied the menu for a moment, then returned his smile with one of her own.

"So, how come you're not married," she asked. "Rich, powerful, handsome - I would think you'd need a bodyguard to keep the girls off you."

"Wow," Mick laughed. "I thought we were sticking with nice, safe subjects for conversation."

The waitress came for their orders just in time to break the awkward silence that followed, as Mackenzie internally chided herself. *What were you thinking, asking a question like that? You barely know the man.*

"The steaks are fabulous here, Mick." Mackenzie said setting her menu aside. Mick deferred to Mackenzie, who ordered a house salad, baked potato, medium rare rib eye and strawberry pie for dessert. He chose the rack of baby back ribs, then waited for the server to refill their tea glasses and leave before answering. It was his turn to grow somber with old memories.

42

"I suppose I have some trust issues when it comes to women," he confessed. The raised eyebrow from across the table indicated that might not have been the best answer. "Present company excepted, of course." He smiled and Mackenzie relaxed a bit. "My grandfather never approved of my father's marriage. He believed my mother only married him for his money. Whether or not that was true, I don't know. I don't remember either of them. But it wouldn't surprise me. I have personally dated girls who I later realized were only interested in my checkbook."

Mick took a long sip of iced tea and collected his thoughts. He wanted to say this right.

"But it's not just the women who are chasing a husband with big bucks. It's men who are driven to succeed and who are willing to sacrifice everything to get to the top. In my business, I see it all the time, wives and kids fall victim to the corporate ladder. I knew I was in line to inherit the family business, and that's a huge responsibility; one I don't take lightly. I hold the fate of literally thousands of employees in my hands. I didn't want to enter into a relationship and not be able to give it my full attention."

The salads arrived and Mick offered Mackenzie his hand. "Is it okay if I give thanks before we eat?"

Mackenzie looked at him and nodded her head. "You are a very special man, Mick Lambert."

The remainder of the meal was spent in light-hearted conversation; good memories and hopes for the future. Mick wasn't sure he had ever been this comfortable with a woman, and Mackenzie felt alternately bold and shy, something she hadn't experienced since her teenage years.

After dinner they drove back to the Austen home in a silence that was satisfying, rather than awkward. Mackenzie waited for Mick to open her car door, much to his surprise, and he escorted her up to the porch.

"Thanks for the meal and the conversation," Mackenzie said. "It's been a long time." The porch light illuminated her red curls, lending her an ethereal, angelic glow. "Remember, you promised me another ride in Gringolet before you go back to the big city," she laughed.

The thought of leaving this town, this woman, hit him like a blow to the stomach. *I don't want to be anywhere that she is not. Where did that thought come from?*

He forced a smile, then nodded his head and raised his fist to his heart in a chivalrous salute. "You have my word, M'lady." He then took her right hand, bowed and brushed the back of her hand with his lips. "Goodnight, Mackenzie. I really enjoyed myself." Then he turned and stepped off the porch toward his car.

Mackenzie stood stunned, her hand still warm from his kiss. She could feel a flush rising up her neck and coloring her cheeks. She entered the house and dropped her purse on the living room sofa.

"Hi everyone; I'm home," she called.

"Hey," Wendy called back, "Come in here and tell us how it went." Wendy patted the cushion beside her on the couch. "Com'on sis, spill."

"There's really nothing to talk about," Mackenzie said, although the color in her cheeks called her a liar. "We had a nice meal, and he said he was coming to church Wednesday night, and he promised to take me for a spin Gringolet before he leaves town."

Bryan shot her a puzzled look. "What in the world is a Gringolet?"

Mackenzie broke into a laugh. "You wouldn't understand. Gringolet is what I call his Corvette. It's a great, hulking beast of a car and I think it's adorable."

"Adorable? You call that thing adorable," her mother asked.

"It's like living next to an airport. That thing shakes the house, it's so noisy."

"Shakes the house," Bryan asked. "Does it need a muffler?"

"Son," John cut in, "it has mufflers, sort of. That car is all motor. It's black and has a red patch on the hood. I think it says '427' on it, and the exhaust pipes are under the doors."

"So, it's a muscle car. What makes it adorable?"

"He treasures that car because his grandfather gave it to him as a graduation present from college."

"Harvard?" Wendy asked.

"Yes. He was driving Gringolet when he took us to the hospital. Now, if you will excuse me, I've had a long day, and I've got another one tomorrow. I'm going to bed." Mackenzie stood and almost skipped down the hall toward her bedroom.

Wendy shook her head, a knowing smile playing across her lips. "I think someone has a serious case of *the likes* for Mr. Mick Lambert."

CHAPTER 10

The morning sounds of the hospital were becoming familiar to Mackenzie; the rhythmic *thump-thump* of carts rolling through the halls, the intercom pages, the hushed, murmured voices of doctors and nurses. *Too familiar,* Mackenzie thought as she stepped off the elevator and onto the Pediatric floor. She instinctively reached for Mick's hand, then bit her lip, realizing she was probably overstepping her boundaries.

If Mick minded, he didn't seem to show it. He held her hand as if it were the most natural thing in the world, two lovers on a stroll through the park. *Only this isn't a park, and I'm not a high school kid on a date. My daughter is in the hospital for crying out loud. Focus, Mackenzie!* she thought. But she didn't let go of Mick's hand.

They entered Morgan's room to find her awake in her bed.

"Hi Baby." Mackenzie smiled broadly and went to pick her up.

"Mommy," the child squealed, reaching up for her mother. After a big hug, Morgan held her finger up for inspection. "Hurt."

Mackenzie took the smaller hand in hers and raised the injured finger to her lips, giving it a Mommy-kiss that makes all things better. At that moment, Morgan noticed the other person in the room.

"Mick!" she called out, and reached for him. Once in Mick's

arms she noticed the embroidery on his shirt. Morgan squealed with delight, clapping and pointing. "Mickey Mouse, Mickey Mouse," she laughed.

"Good morning, Sweet Pea," he said.

Mackenzie reached for Morgan, and whispered to Mick, "How many Mickey Mouse shirts do you have?"

"A few," Mick smiled back.

Mackenzie took Morgan to the bathroom, and by the time they returned, breakfast had arrived. Mother and child sat down on the love seat. Mick pushed the tray in front of them, then sat down out of the way and watched, fascinated as Mackenzie negotiated the challenging task of feeding a toddler scrambled eggs and toast in a valiant attempt to get more food inside the child than on her blouse or the floor.

"So, she would have already had her insulin, right?" he asked.

"Yes," Mackenzie replied. "Once she finishes eating, I'll bathe her and get her dressed. I don't have to be in the conference room for class until nine, so you've got time to grab a cup of coffee if you want."

She smiled at Mick, and his mouth went dry. It took a moment for him to work enough moisture back into his mouth to reply. "Yeah, sure. I'll leave you to do what you do best, and be back in a few."

He rose to leave and give Mackenzie and Morgan some privacy when the sound of her voice stopped him.

"I can't thank you enough," Mackenzie said. "I can't think of any other man, other than maybe my father, who would willingly drop what he was doing to babysit a toddler."

"I have nothing to drop," he smiled. "I'm on vacation, remember?"

"That's my point. You're on vacation. You should be playing

golf, or tennis, or fishing, or whatever. The thing is, I feel a little guilty asking, but do so appreciate it."

He threw back his head and laughed. "I hate golf and I stink at tennis. I do like fishing, though. I tell you what, when this whole thing is over, you can pay me back by heading into the mountains for a little trout fishing. Deal?"

"Deal," Mackenzie laughed, then shooed him out of the room.

By the time Mick returned, Morgan was bathed and dressed in red corduroy jeans and a red and white polka dot tee shirt. Together they walked to the playroom. Morgan squirmed down from Mackenzie's arms and joined the six other youngsters who were coloring at the table. Mackenzie introduced Mick to the duty nurse.

"Ah, so you're him," the nurse said.

"Excuse me?" Mick scrunched his brows together. "I've been called a lot of things in my life, but I'm not sure I've ever been called just, *him*."

"The waiting room incident," the nurse smiled. "The guy with the classic 'Vette and the lady and baby? That's you, right? You're him?"

"Oh, uh, well I suppose I'm guilty. I've come to spend the time with Morgan while mom is in class. Is that okay?"

"It's more than okay. It's great," the nurse replied. She turned to Mackenzie and said in a low whisper, "I knew it was him." She gave Mackenzie a wink, and then walked over to settle a squabble between toddlers.

"See you later Mick, have fun," Mackenzie waved as she disappeared down the hall.

The diabetes class might have been a dull endeavor to a casual observer, but Mackenzie soaked up every word. This was a condition that affected *her* daughter, and she didn't want to miss anything. She listened intently to the nurse educator, taking notes and asking questions whenever she didn't completely understand something. A full day of films, pamphlets and statistics was draining, but satisfying. She learned that treating one so young was more challenging than treating an older patient, but now, armed with knowledge of the hows and whys of juvenile diabetes, she felt encouraged, and even at peace.

It had been a long day. There was really only one thing Mackenzie wanted more than a hot bath and a soft bed was to see Morgan. As she walked the hospital halls toward the Pediatrics ward, her thoughts floated back to dinner date with Mick. Her heart skipped a beat, and she felt that familiar flush rising in her cheeks. She really liked him. *What are you thinking, letting your heart get all tangled with a guy you hardly know? God, You know my judgment with men hasn't been all that great. Please, what am I supposed to do?*

She glanced at her watch as she approached the playroom: 3:30. She stopped outside the door and peeked inside. Cartoon voices, were coming from the room, but the television appeared to be off.

She moved further in through the open door, and stared in amazement at the scene before her. Mick was sitting on a play mat with his back against the wall. Morgan sat in his lap, her back against his chest. A child was under each arm. Two others jammed against him as he read to them in all the different voice, adding the requisite sound effects. The children and Mick were engrossed in the story and didn't notice her entrance.

The nurse smiled at her and quietly walked over. "Does your boyfriend want a job?"

CHAPTER 11

Mick walked back up his driveway after his morning jog. He had slept late; his watch showed ten o'clock. He unlocked the front door and walked in, pausing long enough to drop his keys in the basket on the table by the door, before making his way into the kitchen. He poured a glass of orange juice, and sat down on a stool at the bar. It was strange not having a 'to-do' list controlling his day.

"Let's see," he said out loud, "What shall I do today? I'm already sweaty. Perhaps I should wax Gringolet." He stopped and pondered for a moment. *Why did I call my 'Vette, Gringolet?* Then he laughed at himself. He already knew the answer to that question, and it came in the form of 95-pound red head.

Mick downed the last of his orange juice and headed out to the garage where he retrieved some wax and a chamois. He raised the hood on the classic car first and wiped it down, getting all the accumulated dirt and grime off. Far from considering this drudgery, Mick found it relaxing, a chore he could do by rote. His thoughts turned to his grandfather who would often share these chores with him when he was a boy, quoting scriptures as they worked together, training him up in the way he should go.

He missed those days. *Wish he was here now*, he thought. *He'd know how to find the answers I'm looking for.* Then he sighed, quoting one of his grandfather's favorite saying: *If wishes were wings a frog wouldn't bump his butt.*

Mick smiled to himself, and made a decision. He closed the hood. *Thank you Lord, that You are here.* He picked up his cell phone and entered numbers he knew by heart.

Three rings.

"Gordon Palmer."

"Good morning, Gordon. How's it going?"

"Hey, Mick! Good to hear from you. Boy, do we miss you around here."

Mick laughed out loud, "Gordon, you don't need me underfoot. You can handle it blindfolded. But thanks for saying it. I miss you too."

Palmer had been with Lambert Group for more than 30 years. As long as Mick had known him, Palmer had been his grandfather's right hand man. The only person Palmer answered to now was Mick, and Mick trusted him implicitly.

"I see Lambert Electronics stock is up four points on the year." Mick pulled a stool over and sat down.

"Yeah, we expect to have a great quarter."

Mick made small talk for a few minutes before finally getting to the real purpose of his call. "Gordon, I want you to do something for me."

"Sure Mick. What?"

"Sell Grandfather's house."

Not much surprised Gordon Palmer, but the pause on the other end of the line told Mick this was a blindside.

"Are you sure? That place has been in the family for…well, for a long time."

"I know, Gordon. But I'm a single man with simple tastes. It's just too much. I don't need it, and there's certainly no benefit to paying for all the upkeep, not to mention the exorbitant property taxes, on the place. The fact is, I've been praying about moving for a long time. There's really no reason for me to come into the office every day; no reason I couldn't telecommute and live anywhere I wanted. Honestly, Gordon, I like it here. I'm thinking about buying a place here."

"In Winston, Colorado? What on earth would possess you to do that?"

Mick couldn't tell him those reasons included two redheads. Instead he relied on some peripheral reasoning.

"Look, Gordon, it's beautiful here. It's quiet and peaceful. I can sit on the deck at night before going to bed and meditate. I love it. Anything at the company that requires my input can be done by phone, and I can fly back for board meetings. There is simply no reason I need to be in Connecticut or New York?"

"Okay. Sounds like you've made up your mind. I'll put it on the market. You know that little shack is worth a mint."

Mick smiled at the description of the family estate as a 'little shack,'—a 40-room mansion situated on 50 acres of prime real estate in one of the most exclusive, sought after areas in the county. "Yeah, I know. Do you think it will take long to sell?"

"Hard to say. Bud Alexander has been salivating over that property since before you were born, so probably not."

"Hey, Gordon, be fair on the price, but don't give it away either."

"You're the boss."

"Thanks, Gordon. I can always count on you. If you need me, call." Mick punched his cell phone off and launched into waxing the Corvette.

Mackenzie gave Morgan a quick hug. It was past time for

her afternoon nap, but her sister's family was about to head back to Texas, and they had stopped at the hospital for a final goodbye. "We get to go home in the morning, sweetheart," Mackenzie told her daughter.

The toddled nodded a sleepy smile as she looked around the room. Her grandmother and Aunt were there. Suddenly, as if a cloud had drifted in front of the sun, her face morphed into a mask of abject misery and she began to weep.

"Baby, what's wrong," Mackenzie asked, bewildered.

"Want Mick! Where Mick?" Morgan sobbed.

"Mick?" Mackenzie repeated, completely flabbergasted. "Mick is at his house. You can see him tomorrow at church, okay? He promised he would sit with us."

This was not the answer Morgan was looking for. "Where Mick," She demanded.

"Baby, he can't come right now."

The child began to wail inconsolably.

Mackenzie looked from her mother to her sister, but they looked as helpless as she felt. "How about if I call Mick," she suggested. "Do you want to talk to him on the phone?"

This seemed to have a mollifying affect on the child. Mackenzie fumbled for her purse.

"Here." Darla Austen handed her cell phone to her daughter.

"Thank you," Mackenzie mumbled as she punched numbers into the keypad. The phone rang twice before Mick picked up.

"Mick! Am I glad I caught you!"

"Mackenzie? What's wrong? Is Morgan okay?" He could hear the child still sobbing in the background.

"She's okay; I think she's just really tired. It's past her nap time. But she's upset that she didn't get to see you today. Would you mind just talking to her for a minute or two?"

"Sure. Put her on."

Mackenzie placed the phone to Morgan's ear.

"Hello, Morgan"

"Mick? Mick," Morgan's normal smile returned.

"Hey Morgan. How's my brave girl? I'll see you at church tomorrow."

"Promise?"

Mick felt his heart melt into his shoes. "You've got it, Baby. I promise. I'll see you tomorrow."

"Got it, baby! 'morrow." As if satisfied that all was well with the world, Morgan handed the cell phone back to her mother, and squirmed down to play with her aunt.

Mackenzie came on the line. "I have no idea what you said, but thank you. 'Got it, baby?' What was that all about?"

"Call me tonight when you have more time and I'll tell you all about it."

"Um, okay. Thanks again, Mick." She ended the call and handed the phone back to her mother, who was giving her that familiar, 'We need to talk,' look.

Morgan was snuggled up on her Aunt Wendy's lap and almost asleep. Mackenzie met her mother's gaze and said, "What?"

Darla pursed her lips for a moment, then pitched her voice low to keep from disturbing the toddler.

"Mackenzie, you know I don't mean to interfere in your life, but don't you think that baby is getting a little too wrapped up in Mick? I mean, we all think the world of Mick, but he's only visiting for a while. What happens when he goes home?"

Mackenzie did not want to think about that.

"I'll worry about that when it happens, mom." Darla gave her a dubious look. "He's a good guy. He won't hurt her."

"He may not intend to, Sis, but mom's right," Wendy added

to the conversation. "He lives in Connecticut, right? I mean, that's half way across the country."

"Mick is good for her. Can't you two see that?" Mackenzie looked from her sister to her mother pleadingly.

"No one said he's bad," Darla said. "We just want you to be careful."

"Yeah, Sis. Mick's a great guy," Wendy smiled. "But I'm afraid it won't be just Morgan who get a broken heart when he leaves."

Mackenzie realized she was busted. "Is it really that obvious?"

Darla and Wendy shared a quick glance, then smiled. "Oh, yeah!"

Once Morgan was down for the night, Mackenzie wandered down to the waiting room, grabbed a cup of coffee, and dialed Mick's number. It rang several times, and she was about to hang up when Mick's voice came on the line.

"Hello."

"Hi, Mick."

"Mackenzie. You sound exhausted, or maybe like you've got something weighing on your mind?"

Very perceptive, she thought. "Mick, I really like you, but…"

"But?"

"Here's the deal, Mick - Mom and my sister think that Morgan is getting too attached to you. They are afraid that it will be really hard on Morgan when you leave and go back to Connecticut." *There, I said it.*

There was a pregnant pause on the other end of the line.

"I see. And what about you?"

"What about me?"

"Are your mother and sister worried about you getting too attached to me? And more to the point, are you worried that you are getting too attached to me? Are you afraid that I'm going to hurt you? And Morgan?"

Mackenzie, blew out a deep breath. "Yes."

"I appreciate your honesty, Mackenzie. Is that it? Are there any other problem?"

"Yes. I mean, no," Mackenzie stumbled over her reply. *Why does talking to this guy get me so flustered?* "I mean, yes, that is it, and no, there isn't any other problem."

He chuckled.

"I don't think it's funny."

"No, I don't either. I was just thinking about that old saying, 'if you want to make God laugh, tell Him your plans.'"

"And that's funny because?"

"Mackenzie, I'm not leaving Winston. I'm not going back to Connecticut."

Mackenzie's heart skipped a beat. Maybe two, or three. "I... don't understand. I mean, um...Why?"

"Well, I've always liked Winston and..."

"You've been here before?"

"Yeah. My Grandfather used to bring me here every winter to ski, but I haven't been here for a few years. I like it here. I like your dad's church. And I like you."

Now Mackenzie's heart was beating fast, as if working overtime to make up for those skipped beats.

"So, what would you do about work?"

"They don't need me for the day to day operation of the company. Anything that needs my input can be done by phone or e-mail. I'll have to fly back periodically, but most of the stuff I can handle from anywhere."

"Wait," she said as what he previously said sunk in. "Did you say, you like me?"

Mick smiled. "Yeah, I did. I hope that's okay. And I hope, maybe, you...like me too?"

Mackenzie bit her lower lip to keep from giggling. "Yeah, Mick," she managed. "I like you, too."

"I am glad to hear that," Mick breathed a sigh of relief."

"So, what's with the whole 'Got it, baby' thing?"

Mick burst out laughing. "I told Morgan I would see her at church tomorrow and she wanted me to promise. I did and told her, 'You've got it, Baby.'"

Mackenzie laughed with him. "I think you're a bad influence on my daughter, sir."

"Me? Hey, she's the one who steals hearts. And speaking of stealing hearts, since I'm not moving back to the big city; do you think I could talk her mother into going out with me again sometime?"

Mackenzie paused, then asked, "Why? Why do you want to go out with me?"

"You sound surprised."

"I'm so...average, and you're...well, you are *you*. Surely there are plenty of women who are more your economic equal, who are beautiful and glamorous and..."

Mick cut her off. "Sure. I've dated my share of the glitterati. But I'm not impressed by them. Why do I want to go out with you? I don't know. I just really,,,I like you Mackenzie. You're... real. I hope that's okay."

"Mick, I like you, too." She giggled out loud. "I suppose I could be talked into a date with you. Mick, I'm sorry, I have to go. Mom is calling me. I'll see you at church tomorrow?"

"You've got it, Baby!" He hung up the phone, walked out

on his deck and looked out at the stars in the clear mountain sky. He smiled and bowed his head in prayer of thanksgiving.

CHAPTER 12

The cars in the church parking lot surprised him. *It's Wednesday evening,* Mick thought. *What are all these people doing here?* He parked his car and headed for the sanctuary, and was again surprised by the number of people who stopped to greet him and shake his hand. He stopped in the foyer to take it all in. *It feels…friendly,* he thought, *just like the people in the parking lot.*

He wandered into the sanctuary and allowed his eyes to wander over the crowds until he spotted Mackenzie down front. He tried to work some moisture back into his mouth, that had suddenly gone dry.

Lord have mercy, she's beautiful, he thought. Decked out in white pants topped by a pale green blouse that only accentuated her flaming red hair, Mackenzie was settled on the front pew next to her parents. A multitude of well-wishers were fussing over Morgan, who played around her mother's feet.

Mick started down the aisle, but before he made half the trek, Morgan saw and and shrieked, "Mick!" The toddler bolted toward him as fast as her toddler legs could run, arms stretched wide for him. He bent down and caught her, lifted her up, and hugged her to his chest.

"Missed you, Mick," Morgan said into the side of his neck, and Mick felt his heart swell.

"Missed you too, Baby. How are you feeling?"

"Okay," she said.

When Mick looked up, he was embarrassed to see a huge portion of the congregation staring at him and Morgan with a collective bemused smile.

"Um, hi everyone," he said with a half wave.

"Hi Mick," Mackenzie walked up the aisle to meet him, followed by her father.

"Glad you could make it, Son," the pastor held out his hand and came to his side. "And by the way, if you're not doing anything tomorrow, I'd love to buy you some lunch."

"Sure," Mick answered. "What time?"

"How about noon? There's a great little burger joint down the street. Fresh beef, locally grown fixin's. Actually tastes like real food, unlike some of the stuff sold by those national chains."

"Sounds great. I'll meet you here and we can drive over, if that's okay with you."

The music started, indicating the service was about to begin, and people were taking their seats. It appeared to Mick that most of the people had a regular place, almost like it was reserved for them. There was an empty seat on the front row beside Mackenzie; one that was created when Mackenzie placed Morgan on her lap, and Mick was happy to take that spot.

After several lively praise songs, the worship pastor nodded toward Mackenzie, who passed Morgan to her mother, then climbed the few steps up to the platform. She took a microphone from its stand.

"It's great to be here tonight," she declared as she walked back and forth a little, beaming that infectious smile of hers. "I can't begin to tell you how wonderful I feel. This past week was a difficult time for me. Anybody else have a rough week?"

Hands raised all across the auditorium.

"If you are anything like me, you needed more strength than you have on your own. You needed some prayers going up on your behalf. Am I right?"

A smattering of 'Amens' echoed.

"I want to thank each and every one of you for your prayers. The Lord heard them." She scanned the congregation and waited expectantly, a grin playing around the corners of her mouth. "I don't think you heard what I said. I said, the Lord heard them."

This time the congregation responded to her with laughter, applause and amens.

"That's why I'm here tonight," she said. "To thank Him. To worship Him. To praise Him. That's why I come up here. That's why I sing. God hears us. Just think about that for a moment. The almighty God, the Creator of heaven and earth, the One who commands the sun to rise and says to the waves, 'come this far, and no further,' He…hears…your…prayers! I don't know what you came to do tonight, but I came to praise the Lord!"

She was radiant. Mick would have sworn she was glowing. She took a step forward, closed her eyes, raised the microphone to her lips and began to sing. And Mick thought all of heaven held its breath.

"And I sing because I'm happy. And I sing because I'm free."

The hair on the back of Mick's neck stood up. He had never heard anything so beautiful.

"His eye is on the sparrow…" voices from across the auditorium began to join in until the whole room was filled with reverential praise. It was breathtaking.

"And I know, I know He watches me."

She lowered the microphone and a hushed silence reigned for several moments as a holy expectation began to build. Mackenzie raised her left hand toward the sky and with tears in her eyes began to sing 'The Old Rugged Cross' accapella. Morgan patted Mick's arm. He smiled down at the toddler. She leaned close to him, pointed at her mother, then whispered, "Mommy sings pretty."

Mick whispered back, "Yes, Baby. She sure does."

The congregation worshipped as one for a few more moments, then broke into smaller groups for Bible study and prayer. Mick was engrossed. He loved God, and was raised in the church, but he had not experienced this kind of community before. He thought the service ended much too soon, but when he looked at his watch it was already 9:00 o'clock.

Mackenzie found him on his way out of the building. Morgan, was snuggled up in her arms with a sleepy head against her shoulder.

"Thanks for coming," she said. "I hope you enjoyed it."

"Mackenzie…" he breathed.

"Call me 'Mac,'" she grinned.

"Mac," he complied. "I heard you sing on Sunday, so I knew you were good. I just had no idea how good. You are fantastic! Have you ever thought of recording?"

Mackenzie laughed out loud, then cocked her head to the side, studying him with those startling green eyes. "You're kidding, right?"

"No, I am not."

She reached up and patted him on the cheek.

"You're sweet, Mick, but look at me," she nodded to the child in her arms. "Do I look like a rock star to you? I'm a single mother. Honestly, I'm perfectly happy to sing in my church. God is the one who gave me the gift. I only sing for Him."

"Fine. Don't be a rock star. Don't even be a country star. Record Christian music. They do that these days, you know."

"Thank you, for your business advice," she quipped. "But, before I sign my contract, I need to put this little one to bed. See you tomorrow?"

"You've got it, Baby," he grinned. "Now if you'll excuse me, I have a date to plan. Dinner and a good movie perhaps?"

"Well, dinner at least. Give me a call tomorrow afternoon and we'll firm things up."

"Can I carry Morgan to your car?"

Mackenzie nodded assent, and they transferred the sleeping child into Mick's arms.

He buckled her in the car seat, then escorted Mackenzie to the driver's side.

"Well, goodnight," he said, extending his hand."

Mackenzie surprised him by taking his hand and drawing him into a brief hug. He felt his heart beating faster in his chest. "Well, that was nice," he said as they broke apart. He bent low over her hand and brushed it with a kiss.

"You know, I could get used to all of this chivalry," she giggled.

"Drive carefully, M'lady," he admonished as she climbed behind the wheel. Then he stood to the side and watched her drive away.

CHAPTER 13

At twelve o'clock Mick pulled into the Faith Center parking lot. He walked to the church office and entered. Mrs. Shields, the church secretary, looked up and flashed a genuine smile. "May I help you?"

"Hi. I'm Mick Lambert. I had a meeting with Pastor Austen.

"Yes, you do," the secretary did a quick scan of her calendar, then said brightly, "Yes, you do. The pastor is expecting you. Go on in."

Mick gave a questioning look, and Mrs. Shields pointed at an office two doors down the hall, on the left. Mick nodded, and headed that direction. He rapped lightly, and after a muffled 'come in,' opened the door.

"Hello, Mick," John smiled. "Have a seat. I'll be ready in just a moment."

"Thank you, sir."

"Back in my Army days I would have said, 'I'm not a 'sir.' I work for a living,'" the pastor laughed. "Don't be so formal, Mick. Call me John." He shuffled some paper into the Out box on his desk and stood. "Ready. Hope you're hungry. I could eat a horse."

"Sure. Shall I drive?"

"Did you bring the beast with you?"

"No, I didn't," he laughed."

"That's too bad. But sure, you drive." John told his secretary he would be back in an hour and walked with Mick to the parking lot. He waited until the Mercedes was on the street and rolling toward the restaurant before addressing the issue at hand.

"I guess you're wondering why I want to see you," John began. Without waiting for an answer he continued. "A little bird told me you are planning on staying in Winston, maybe even making it your permanent residence."

"Well, I…"

"I think that's fine," the pastor continued. "I had a chat with the elders, and, well, with your considerable experience in the field, we were wondering if you might consider sharing some of your financial wisdom with our finance committee, you know, be something of a consultant."

"Well, I…"

The pastor waved his hand. "I'm not trying to twist any arms here. I know you're on vacation and you don't really have any ties to our little body of Believers, but I know you're a Christian, and I'm a pretty good judge of character. I trust you. I know handling money is your strong suite. You're good at it. You have business sense, and you have integrity."

"Well, I…"

"Turn here," John pointed to a hole in the wall storefront with a neon sign that flashed, "Jake's Place."

Mick hit his turn signal and pulled into the parking lot.

"We need your expertise," the pastor said as they entered the restaurant. "Afternoon, Judy," he said as a large woman in her 50s escorted them to a corner booth.

"You need a menu, John, or are you gonna have the usual," Judy asked.

"Oh, the usual for me, Judy."

"Why do I even ask? How 'bout you, young feller? You need a menu?"

"Well, I…"

"I recommend the usual," John said.

"Alright," Mick acquiesced. "I'll have the usual."

Judy nodded and waddled away.

"Pastor…"

"John, please."

"John," Mick nodded. "I'm happy to offer any wisdom I might have, but I have absolutely no knowledge of your church's financial picture. Is the church in trouble? Do you have a specific financial need?"

Judy waddled back to the table and placed two mason jars filled with iced tea in front of the men. Then she disappeared back into the kitchen.

John smiled. "Good questions. No we're not in trouble and we don't have any particular financial need right now. God has been very good to us. As far as getting to know the church's financial picture, that is easily remedied. There's a meeting of the finance committee tomorrow morning. If you want to come by we'll open up our books and you can take a good, hard look."

Judy appeared once again carrying to plates loaded with the biggest hamburgers Mick had ever seen, and enough French fries to feed a small Belgian village.

"Holy cow!"

"It will be once we bless it," John laughed. "You want to do the honors?"

The two men bowed their heads and Mick offered thanks for the meal. John dipped a French fry into a puddle of catsup and popped it into his mouth, and Mick wrapped his hands around the burger. They made small talk as they ate, talking about everything from the Broncos' chances for another Super Bowl, to the gorgeous spell of weather the community was enjoying.

"So, what's the next step," Mick asked. He was surprised to realize he had polished off that entire monstrous meal. *Got to do some serious working out to overcome those calories,* he thought, *but man, it was worth it!*

"Just show up tomorrow. I'll let the committee know to expect you. Nine o'clock at the church. So, how'd you like 'the usual?' Not bad, huh?"

Mick sipped his iced tea and patted his belly. "Not bad at all." He paused for a moment, unsure of how to broach the subject that had been on his mind since the night before. He decided the direct approach was best. "Can I ask you something, John?"

"Fire away," the older man replied.

"Mackenzie has a fantastic voice, and an incredible stage presence. Has she ever thought about recording a CD?"

John smiled broadly. "Mackenzie certainly does have a lovely voice, and as far as stage presence, well, we usually call that 'being anointed.' But as far as doing it professionally, I don't know. I think her heart is really in teaching."

"Probably," Mick nodded. "But don't you think there are a multitude of people out there who don't go to your church, who would be blessed by Mackenzie's…anointing?"

Now it was John's turn to say, "Well, I…"

"I know some people in the industry. Do you think anyone would object if I made a phone call?"

"I don't think anyone would object," John pondered the possibilities for a moment. "Mackenzie is certainly talented, and she is such a blessing to everyone who knows her."

"That she is."

"I think you might want to ask her first, though."

"Probably a good idea. That girl does seem to have a mind of her own," Mick laughed.

"Unless I miss my bet, you're a bit smitten with her."

"Well, I…"

John laughed. "That's fine. No need to explain. I had the same look on my face for a year after I met Darla. It still sneaks up on me from time to time."

The image of Mackenzie's face came to Mick's mind, so vibrant and beautiful. "Honestly, I'm not sure how I feel about Mackenzie. When I'm around her, everything gets all jumbled up. I feel alive and needed; and I feel small and insignificant; and I feel…oh, I don't know. I've never felt like like this before. My heart beats harder when I see her. She makes me feel strong and weak at the knees at the same time. I want to protect her and Morgan and…"

John wiped his glasses on a napkin. "Sounds like you have it bad, Son. Does she know?"

Mick shook his head. "She's a woman," he said. "Who knows what she knows or doesn't know; or knows and pretends she doesn't know."

John nodded. "Yep. She's her mother's daughter alright." John's demeanor turned stern. "I just have one rule. Don't hurt her. She is a wonderful woman, and she's been hurt enough by men to last a lifetime."

Mick looked him directly in the eye. "Yes sir," was all he said.

Mick reached for the check, but John grabbed it first. "You can get it next time," he smiled. "This one's on me."

Once they were back in the Mercedes, Mick reached into his shirt pocket, pulled out a folded piece of paper and handed it to John.

"What's this," he asked as he unfolded it.

"My tithe check," Mick replied as he pulled into traffic. "I figure if this is going to be my home church, this is where I should be giving my money. Something wrong?"

"Well, most folks tithe on a weekly or monthly basis, as they get paid. We don't usually get a tithe check for a whole year's worth of income."

Mick grimaced a bit.

"That is a weekly tithe," he said.

"Seriously?" The pastor whistled. "You really that rich?"

"Yep."

John stared at him, then at the tithe check, then back at Mick.

"I'd appreciate it if you kept that information to yourself, Mick said. "This kind of information makes people look at me, well, differently, if you know what I mean."

"As you wish," John replied. He took one more look at the check and whistled again. "I'm not sure I've ever seen that many zeroes on one check before."

CHAPTER 14

The meeting at church with the finance committee was a success. Mick sat in the back of the room and listened as the committee took care of business. He was impressed with their discipline and efficiency. *Our board of directors could take a lesson from these guys,* he thought.

Up for discussion were plans for additions to the academy, a proposal for increasing teacher pay and a request to increase the size and scope of the church's community food pantry. The committee accepted all the plans.

John had already introduced Mick, but now the pastor invited him to address the committee. Each member directed their full attention to the newcomer. Mick cleared his throat, thanked them for the warm welcome and gave them a brief overview of his background, which appeared to be completely unnecessary, as the pastor had already prepped the committee members. If anyone seemed overly impressed, they didn't show it. To them, Mick was just another one of the members of their body of believers. Mick found it refreshing.

Once the meeting adjourned, he received a half-dozen invitations for coffee, and made arrangements to meet each one. He spent the next couple of hours going over the church's financial records with the church bookkeeper, and found them to be concise and impeccably well kept. As John had indicated, the church was in good financial shape, able to meet all of its obligations, give away significant amounts to meet local needs and still have enough left over to provide support for several missionaries.

While the church was doing plenty of things right, Mick made mental notes of a few things they could do to keep the church on sound financial footing when those inevitable rough patches hit. When he mentioned them to John, the pastor just smiled.

"I knew there was something I liked about you," the older man said. "I'll bring your suggestions up to the finance committee next month. Unless, of course, you'd like to come and make the suggestions yourself. Which would probably be a good idea. No sense getting information second hand when you can get it straight from the horse's mouth."

CHAPTER 15

The lazy days of summer drifted by in Winston, Colorado. Morgan was responding well to her diabetes treatments; Mackenzie continued to enthrall Mick with her impish laugh and angelic voice. Gordon Palmer had The Lambert Group hitting on all cylinders, and he had just closed on his new home the week before. Mick chuckled to himself and shook his head. It wasn't quite fair that one man could be so incredibly fortunate, but Mick didn't take it for granted. He knew the source of his good fortune, and took time to acknowledge the Giver of all good gifts.

Thank you Lord. You have been so very good to me, he prayed as he gazed out the tall windows overlooking the pristine valley below. *Help me to be faithful to administer all You've given me in a way that pleases you.*

Mick spent the morning working in his yard, planting rose bushes to accent the front entry way. Of course he could have hired a local landscaping firm to do the manual labor, but he relished the hard work. *But after all,* he thought, *this is my house now; I should put my own sweat into making it a home.*

He had overheard Mackenzie telling her mother how much she loved roses, and putting them in just seemed like the right thing to do.

Now he was taking a break and enjoying the fruit of his labor. He had grabbed a cold Dr. Pepper from the fridge and was sipping it from the bottle as he admired the view when his reverie was interrupted by the ring tone from his cell.

"Hello?"

"Mick. When you coming to see me?" The childish voice on the phone made him smile.

"Well, hello Miss Morgan. I don't know when I'm coming to see you. I haven't been invited."

"Okay. See you tomorrow."

"Umm…"

There was the sound of a slight struggle, and a new voice came on the line.

"Hi, Mick," Mackenzie said. "Sorry about that. Morgan got into my purse and hit the speed dial on my cell phone."

Mick chuckled. "So, you've got me on speed dial, huh? I've made the big time!"

"Don't get the big head," Mackenzie admonished. "I've got my dentist on speed dial too, and you know how much I like going to the dentist."

Mick laughed again, and after some playful banter he said, "Actually, I'm glad Morgan called. It saves me the trouble. I've gotten all moved into my new place, and I'd love to have a few folks over, you know, as kind of a housewarming party. I wondered if you and your folks might want to come over for a cook out tomorrow? I'm pretty handy with a grill, and there's a picnic table in the backyard. What do you think? Hamburgers and hot dogs, maybe some grilled veggies for our vegan friends?"

"It sounds great, but let me ask Mom if they are free." Mick heard a brief muffled conversation, then Mackenzie was back. "Okay, we're on! What time?"

"Your call, Mac. What's better for you, lunch or dinner? I don't want to interfere with Morgan's nap time."

"Aw, that's kind of you, thinking of Morgan," Mackenzie was genuinely touched. Most of the men she had encountered since her husband's death viewed her child as an imposition, something to be put up with. Yet this man was taking Morgan's needs into consideration. "Mmm, let's do lunch. She'll run out of steam in the afternoon and go down for a nap, and we then can enjoy some quiet."

"OK, tell Morgan I'll see her tomorrow."

"Here, tell her yourself."

A childish voice took over the phone, bringing a grin to Mick's face.

"Hey Morgan. You want to come to my house tomorrow?"

"You got it, Baby," Morgan replied, bringing a laugh to both Mick and Mackenzie, who came back on the line.

"Did you get that, *Baby?*"

"Yes, you can stop the snickering now." Not that he wanted her to.

I love her laugh, he thought as he hung up the phone. *In fact, I feel like I'm beginning to love everything about her.*

He took a long swig of Dr. Pepper, the memory of green eyes and red hair wafting through his mind, then headed for the shower to wash away the sweat from the morning's work.

CHAPTER 16

Eleven thirty; they'll be here soon. Mick brushed his hair then splashed on a little aftershave. He pulled a white polo shirt on over his jeans, and examined the effect in his cheval mirror. *Does this look okay? Too casual? Maybe I should... Dude! Calm down. What are you so nervous about? Annnd, now I'm talking to myself. No, seriously. Calm down. It's only Mackenzie. Only Mackenzie! Wow, that's like comparing the Mona Lisa to a paint by number kit.*

The doorbell chime. *You can do this!* He took one last look in the mirror and sighed. *This is as good as it's gonna get.* He walked from his bedroom to the front door, opened it and greeted his guests.

"I see my directions were good. Come in." He welcomed Darla, shook hands with John and gave a Mackenzie a quick hug before reaching down for Morgan.

"This is beautiful. What a lovely house," Darla exclaimed. Prior to her marriage, she had studied interior design, and she had an eye for quality details. She was like a kid in a candy store as she took in the elegantly appointed great room.

"Wow!" was all Mackenzie could say. She looked at the beamed high ceilings, the polished hardwood floors, the marble fireplace in the corner. She imagined snuggling up in front of that fireplace on a cold winter's evening.

"You like it?"

"I love it!" Mackenzie said.

"Let me show you my favorite part of this house," Mick said as he led the Austens through the kitchen to a lovely set of French doors that opened onto a balcony with a breathtaking view of the town and the surrounding countryside.

Darla stepped to the railing and paused a moment to enjoy the vista that spread out before her. "Have you ever seen anything so beautiful," she breathed.

Her husband walked up behind her and put his arms around her waist. He gazed out toward the horizon.

"God's handiwork. It doesn't get any more beautiful," John said.

"Look, Morgan," Mackenzie pointed down the mountainside. "See way down there? We live down there."

Morgan clapped her hands and giggled as she pointed. "Down dere?"

Mick took a moment to enjoy the tableau. There really wasn't anything quite like the bond of a close family. Then he said, "I'll give you the grand tour later. Right now, everyone out back. That's where all the food is."

Mick led them down the stairs and into the back yard where the grill was already hot. "Hey ladies," he smiled. "I love the mother-daughter outfits." Mackenzie and Morgan were indeed matched up in khaki shorts, white sleeveless pullovers and white sandals. "Very chic!"

"I used to hate it when mom would make me and Wendy dress alike when we were kids, and I swore I'd never do that to my child," Mackenzie laughed. "But now; well, things are different when you are a parent. Now I think it's the coolest thing in the world to wear matching outfits with my daughter. There may come a day when Morgan hates it, but right now, I'm really enjoying myself."

"I think it's adorable," Mick said. Then he just looked at her and smiled. Mackenzie's heart started beating faster. She felt a blush start to creep up her neck and onto her checks.

Oh, Lord. Not now. Please not now!

"Thank you," she managed to say.

"Goodness, Mick, you have enough food here for Cox's Army," Darla declared, breaking the spell of the moment.

Mrs. Austen surveyed the picnic table. Potato salad, salad, baked beans, with steaks and hot dogs waiting for the grill, chips, two kinds of pies, a cooler of sodas plus a large pitcher of iced tea.

"Everything is sugar-free, so don't worry about Morgan."

"Son, let me man that grill for you," John said with a gleam in his eye.

"I didn't invite you out here to cook."

"Oh, that wasn't a request," the older man replied. "Just ask Darla. If I hadn't been called to preach, I believe I would have been a chef. Stand back, and prepare to be amazed!"

Mackenzie and Darla shrugged and smiled.

"Dad does love to cook," Mackenzie said. "Hey, want to help me with Morgan? I need to check her blood sugar." She focused her attention on Morgan, who was busy chasing butterflies and in general having a great time being a two year-old. "Morgan, come here, Baby!"

Morgan giggled and came running. "Here," the toddler handed her mom a tiny yellow flower, plucked from a rogue dandelion.

"Thank you, sweetie," Mackenzie smiled as she put it in her pocket. "I'll save it for later. Are you ready for your finger stick?" She knew the answer already. Morgan frowned. "Show Mick how brave you are, okay?"

Morgan held out her finger, looked at Mick and began to buzz.

"Buzzz, Buzzz, Buzzzz!"

"That's my brave girl," Mick smiled at her.

Mackenzie swiped an alcohol prep on the tiny finger and pressed the lancet injector to her finger. "That's it. All done." Mackenzie wiped her finger again. "What a brave girl you are. How brave? This much!"

Mackenzie threw her arms out wide, and Morgan copied her movements. She surprised Mick and threw her arms wide open.

"Looks like you need a teensy bit of insulin," Mackenzie told her daughter.

"May I," Mick asked.

"You know how?" Mackenzie cocked her head in surprise. He nodded his head.

"Gordon's son, James, is diabetic. We hung out together as kids. I gave him injections lots of time; subcutaneous, straight in."

Mackenzie held the syringe and alcohol prep. "Be my guest, Dr. Lambert. The easiest place seems to be in her tummy."

"Come here, little sweetie," Mick said to Morgan. "Can I give you your insulin?"

Morgan imitated her mom by tilting her head and looked at him. Finally, she came to him. She pulled her shirt up so Mick could swipe it her tummy with the alcohol swab.

"Okay, Morgan, here we go, time to be brave." A quick short push and it was over. He put a little pressure on the injection site to make sure it would absorb properly, then handed the used syringe to Mackenzie.

Additional guests arrived, many bringing their favorite dishes turning the cookout into a potluck. John relished his role as a short-order cook, flipping burgers, grilling hot dogs and chicken strips, and even serving up some grilled veggies. The laughter was genuine and the fellowship was as warm as the sunshine.

After the meal, Mackenzie put Morgan down for a nap. Mick's other guests began to drift away one by one until only the Austen's were left. They retired to the living room where they enjoyed the opportunity to engage in some quiet conversation.

Mackenzie snapped her fingers, as if she had just remembered something. "Mick. Where is Gringolet? I want to see Gringolet!"

"She's in the garage," Mick said. "Would you like to see her, too Darla? I'd be happy to take you for a ride." He stood and extended his hand toward Darla.

"You two go visit that beast," Darla smiled. "John and I are perfectly fine right here."

Mick led Mackenzie through the kitchen and laundry room and into the garage. He flipped a light switch, and motioned. "After you."

Mackenzie walked around the Corvette. She whistled. "Wow, she's gorgeous!"

Mick opened the driver's side door and said, "Climb in." Mackenzie got in behind the wheel.

"Can you drive a stick?"

"Afraid not."

"I'll have to teach you sometime. She really is an experience to drive."

"You might regret it," she laughed, sending a thrill down Mick's spine. "Once I get her out on the road, I might never bring her back."

Mick placed his forearms on the open window and leaned forward. "You look completely natural behind the wheel," he said. She turned to face him and found her face within inches of his. Her breath caught in her chest, and she involuntarily leaned toward him. As if magnetized, Mick leaned forward at the same time and pressed his lips to hers. Mackenzie put her hand behind his head and held him there as she kissed him back.

They broke apart, taking a moment for each to recover their thoughts.

"I didn't intend to do that, but I can't say sorry," Mick finally confessed.

Mackenzie cocked her head and gave him that coquettish grin of hers. "Good," she said. "I'm not sorry either. Still, we probably should get back inside. Don't want to start any tongues to wagging, do we?"

Back in the living room, the young couple were met with knowing glances from Mackenzie's parents.

"We were beginning to think you got lost," John grinned. Mick started to stammer an explanation, but Darla interrupted him.

"Leave them alone, John," she admonished her husband. "I'm sure it just takes a lot of time to examine a car."

"It's adorable, mom," Mackenzie said.

"If you say so, dear."

They talked for a few more minutes, then Mick said, "I do have one more room I'd like to show you."

He led the party down the hall to the other side of the house and opened the door to the music room. A Steinway baby grand piano dominated the center of a room that could only be described as elegant. The burled walnut paneled walls were accented with tasteful works of art. A crystal chandelier lighted the room, and the hardwood floor was covered in a thick dove grey rug. In one corner stood a concert pedal harp, its gold brilliance contrasting perfectly with the simple dark blue overstuffed sofa and chair.

As gorgeous as the room was, what Mackenzie found the most fascinating was the view. The exterior wall was a series of cathedral windows that offered a spectacular view of the home's lush lawn and English manor style rose garden. In the distance the sun was setting the purplish-blue mountains on fire.

Breathtaking, Mackenzie thought.

"Oh Mick! This is wonderful; a perfect room to write music in. If that view doesn't inspire you to write, nothing will."

"I'd love to hear you play something," Mick replied.

Mackenzie grinned and nodded. She went to the piano and allowed her fingers caress the keys. She closed her green eyes and began to play.

John and Darla had taken a seat on the sofa. Mick leaned on the Steinway and smiled. Mick thought, *Beautiful. Simply beautiful.* He wasn't sure if his thoughts were for the way Mackenzie played, for the way Mackenzie looked, or for the way Mackenzie made him feel.

CHAPTER 17

Mick climbed the stairs to the sanctuary. "I'm telling you Rob, you will not believe what you are about to hear."

Robert Mann slapped him on the back. "We shall see. I only hope she's half as good as you tell me."

The two men made their way to the front where the musicians were warming up. Mick stopped multiple times to greet recently made friends and to introduce Rob. He caught Mackenzie's eye and she walked to the edge of the platform.

"Good morning, Mick," she grinned, cocking her head in that familiar way that always caused his heart to beat faster.

"Hi, Mac," he responded. "I didn't want to interrupt your preparation, but I did want to introduce you to my friend, Robert Mann."

"You just missed Morgan. She's already gone to the nursery." She extended her hand and smiled warmly. "I'm pleased to meet you, Rob. Hope we have a chance to chat after service. Well grab a seat, I gotta go."

Mackenzie resumed her place with the worship team while Mick and Rob found a place to sit. A few moments later the service began. Corporate worship was alternately lively and reverential, ranging from contemporary praise songs to familiar hymns. At last the moment Mick was waiting for arrived. Mackenzie stepped forward to take the microphone.

Mick elbowed Rob in the ribs and whispered, "Hang on to your hat, my friend. You aren't going to believe this."

Mackenzie held the microphone gently, her head bowed in prayer. Then she raised her eyes and gazed across the auditorium. "We serve an awesome God," she whispered, in a voice that seemed to fill the room. She nodded to the musicians, and one sweet, low note rumbled from the cello and hung in the air. Mackenzie brought the microphone to her lips, and worshipped.

It was as if a cloud of glory descended upon the congregation. Some stood with their arms raised. Others sat quietly, their heads bowed in reverential prayer. A few wept. And when she finished singing, Mackenzie placed the microphone back on its stand and sat down next to her mother, as if nothing out of the ordinary had just happened.

Mick elbowed his friend in the ribs again. "Told you," he said.

Rob just nodded.

The sweet spirit that had settled over the congregation as Mackenzie sang, remained during the rest of the service. As soon as it was over, Mackenzie left the auditorium to pick up Morgan. Mick approached her parents.

"This is my friend Robert Mann," he said, making introductions all around. "John, I wonder if you might have some time to talk this afternoon? I know Rob has some thoughts he'd like to share with you."

"Of course," the pastor responded. "Darla's making fried chicken. Why not come over the house for lunch?"

"We wouldn't want to impose."

"Nonsense. No imposition at all," Darla replied."

"Mick! Mick," a tiny voice interrupted the conversation. Morgan ran to him and threw her arms around his legs.

"Well, hello there, Baby. How's my big girl?" Mick picked the toddler up and tickled her tummy. "I'm coming to your house for lunch. Is that okay with you?"

"You've got it, Baby!" Morgan replied, and everyone laughed.

"I didn't know you were coming over," Mackenzie shot Mick a questioning look. "What's going on?"

"It's a surprise," Mick winked. "I think a very nice surprise."

"Then let's get going," Mackenzie said. "I've never been very good at waiting for surprises."

A short time later they were settling into the Austen's living room, while Darla bustled about making sure everyone felt at home. She had made all the preparations for the meal prior to leaving for service, and soon had the table set with fried chicken, mashed potatoes, hot rolls and a lovely tossed salad. John offered thanks and after a hearty "Amen," began to pass the dishes around the table.

After what she considered a polite amount of small talk, Mackenzie finally demanded, "Alright Mick. What was so important that you had to invite yourself over for dinner?"

"Wow," Mick answered with mock indignation. "You really aren't good with surprises, are you?" Everyone at the table laughed, knowing just how true that statement was. "Alright, here's the scoop," he continued. "I asked Robert to join me for service this morning. I wanted him to hear Mackenzie sing."

"I don't understand," Mackenzie said.

"Well, Robert is not just a friend. He's the CEO of Solar Music."

Mackenzie stopped with her fork halfway to her mouth. "Solar Music? As in, Solar Records out of Nashville? Why would you fly all the way from Nashville, just to hear me sing?"

"Mick is more than just an old friend, Mackenzie," Rob said. "We actually used to be in a band together back in high school." Mackenzie felt her eyebrows raise. "He was the guy who always had the best ear for music. I can't tell you how many times we'd go to a concert with an unknown artist, and he'd point to the singer and say, 'She's gonna be a star,' and more often than not he was right. Bottom line; I've learned to trust Mick's instincts. When he tells me I need to hear someone sing, I have no reservations about hopping in the next plane. I'm happy to say in this case, Mick is absolutely right. You, Ms. Austen, are a star in the making. I'd love the opportunity to talk to you about a recording contract."

Mackenzie placed her fork on her plate, then placed her hands in her lap. She tried to say something, but found herself unable to formulate any words.

At last Darla broke the silence. "Oh my," she exclaimed.

"I... uh... I don't know what to say," Mackenzie finally managed.

"I know it's a lot to take in," Rob chuckled. "And I don't expect an immediate answer. I'll have our attorney draw up our standard contract and send it over for your people to look over."

"My people?" Now it was Mackenzie's turn to laugh. "Since when do I have *people*?" Everyone one around the table joined in the laughter.

Rob fished into his wallet, pulled out a business card and handed it to Mackenzie. "I wish I had more time to enjoy your lovely family and this beautiful community, but duty calls. I have to be in the Ft. Worth office in the morning. My direct line's on the card. If you have any questions or concerns about the contract, feel free to call." He shook Mackenzie's hand then turned back to Mick. "I can't understand how such a big voice comes from such a little lady. Okay, buddy, I got a flight to catch."

Mick said his goodbyes to the Austen family, then drove his friend to the airport. On the way back to his home, his cell phone rang. It was Mackenzie.

"Hey Mac, what's up?"

"I'm not sure," Mackenzie replied with a nervous laugh. I think I just…" her voice trailed off.

"Mackenzie? What's wrong?" Mick demanded

"I'm terrified," she admitted in a low voice.

"Of what?"

Mackenzie's words tumbled over each other as she poured out her heart over the cell phone.

"I'm not a professional singer. What am I even thinking about? I've never recorded a song, much less a whole CD. What if I'm terrible? What if people hate me? What if I make an album and nobody buys it? And I have a daughter. Who's going to take care of her while I'm busy trying to be a rock star?"

"Whoa, whoa, whoa! Slow down, little Missy. What-ever happened to *I can do all things through Christ which strengthens me*?"

"Don't you start quoting scriptures at me, Mick Lambert," she huffed. "I know them better than you do."

"Oh, yeah?" he replied. "Well, how 'bout this one: *Perfect love casts out fe*ar. Hey Mac. It's okay to be a little scared. But you are amazing at what you do. So you aren't a professional. Big deal. When you graduated with your degree in education, you weren't a professional until you were hired by a school, right? You become a professional by doing. Being a professional singer is no different."

There was silence on the other end of the line for so long Mick began to wonder if the call had been dropped. At last he heard Mackenzie's voice again.

"Michael David Lambert IV! How did you become so smart?"

"I'm not sure," he laughed. "Great genes, I guess."

"Now you're making me laugh again. If I decide to do this,

and that's a big if, will I have to travel in a bus and live out of a suitcase? 'Cause that's kind of a deal breaker for me."

"A wise man once told me, What's mine is mine and what's yours is subject to negotiation," Mick replied. "Rob is a good guy. Just be honest about what the label can expect from you, travel wise. Negotiate the deal you want, and if it doesn't work, then don't sign the contract."

"I can't believe how excited I am about this opportunity," Mackenzie said. "But I'm afraid I want to do it just because I want to do it. And if I'm going to do it I want it to be because that's what the Lord wants me to do. Does that make any sense at all?"

Mick smiled, imaging a head full of red curls bobbing up and down. "It makes perfect sense," he replied. "Just pray about it. And I'll be praying for you."

CHAPTER 18

Mick lengthened his stride as he hit the last mile home home. Running made him feel good and it gave him time to think, to clear his head and to hear God more clearly. He broke into a sprint for the final 100 yards, then slowed as he neared his driveway. He came to a walk, breathing hard, and give himself a few minutes to cool down before heading back into the house. He made his way to the kitchen and poured a glass of juice. His phone rang as he plopped into a chair.

"Hello?"

"Good morning. It's me, Mick."

"And I'm so glad it's you," Mick grinned. He found it strange how familiar Mackenzie's voice had become. "How are you this morning?"

"I want to let you know I called Mr. Mann."

"And?"

"I hope you understand, Mick. I turned him down. Are you angry?"

"Angry? Why would I be angry?"

"You went to a lot of trouble on my behalf, and I turned it down."

"Hey, Ms. English teacher, remember Polonius? That whole 'to thine own self be true,' right?"

"Thank you for believing in me," Mackenzie breathed. "I want to sing, but not on the road. I couldn't do it. You know what; you asked me once what I want. Well, what I want is to take care of Morgan. I would gladly give up teaching to stay home with her. Big letdown, huh? I'm not a social climber. I told you that I like being a mother, a homemaker. I'm happy in that role. I'm happy singing to, and for, God; but I don't really care anything about singing to, and for, people. Do you understand, Mick?"

There was dead air on the line for a moment, and Mick started to get a bad feeling in the pit of his stomach. Mackenzie let out a deep sigh.

"And...I could never be a corporate wife. I'm just not..."

"Mackenzie, I know you're trying to say something, I'm just not sure what it is."

"I'm a simple person, Mick," Mackenzie answered. "I'm not telling you goodbye, but I think we need time to think about things."

Mick's mouth felt like a bucket of sand. He couldn't speak.

"Are you there, Mick?"

Mick managed to work some moisture back into his mouth.

"Uh, yeah. I'm here." But he felt that a part of him wasn't. "I'm sorry. I didn't mean to upset you. I just thought..."

"I'm not upset. I'm just...I don't really know what I am right now. I think I just need time to think. Bye, Mick."

Mick sat in stunned silence, staring at the phone. Never in a million years had he envisioned this scenario. Now what, Lord? He sat on the deck and allowed his thoughts and emotions to wash over him until the sun set, then he sat there in the darkness, hoping to hear some voice from on high, telling him what to do.

The voice didn't come, and he finally went to bed, and shared the night with restless dreams.

The dawn broke, cheerful and sunny, as if Mick's world hadn't just crumbled around his feet. He followed his normal routine: a brisk five-mile run, coffee on the deck with his Bible and time to pray. But he couldn't concentrate. When he could stand it no longer he reached for his phone and dialed Mackenzie's number. His call went straight to voice mail. He frowned in frustration, then dialed a different number.

"Winston Faith Center."

"Hi, Mrs. Shields. This is Mick Lambert. May I speak to Pastor Austen?"

"Just a moment, Mick."

"This is John Austen."

"Good morning, sir. I need help."

"What can I do for you, Son?"

"I don't know exactly. I mean, I don't know what happened. I thought I was trying to help, but I must have overstepped some invisible boundary that I didn't know even existed, and now Mackenzie isn't answering her phone, and…"

"Mackenzie's not here, Mick."

"Sir? What do you mean, she's not here? Where is she?"

"She decided she wanted to visit her sister for a bit before school starts. She, Morgan and Darla left for Dallas this morning."

Mick felt his heart sink in his chest.

"Oh," he replied. "She said she needed time to think. I just didn't think she needed to think in a different state."

Silence filled the line for an interminable moment.

"Mick, do you love her?"

Mick's eyes burned and a tear dropped in his lap.

"Yes sir, I do," he whispered.

"I already knew that," John said. "But I wasn't sure if you knew it or not."

He paused, gathering his thoughts. "Here's what I suggest: Give her what she asked for – time to think."

Mick nodded into the phone.

"Between you and me, Mackenzie is still getting over Jared."

Mick felt a sudden flare of jealously burn in his soul.

"Jared? But I thought…"

"I don't mean she's still carrying a torch," John continued. But you don't marry someone without giving them a piece of your soul. There still a lot of hurt and guilt and stuff Mackenzie has to work through before she is ready to give her whole heart to anyone. Listen, Mick. I believe you love Mackenzie and Morgan. But the real test of love is patience. Remember, love is patient and kind, and it never, ever gives up. You say you love her. This is your chance to prove it."

Mick nodded into the phone again.

"Thank you, John."

Mick disconnected the call, and made a decision. He dressed, packed a suitcase, stopped by the realtor's office, then he caught a cab to the airport.

CHAPTER 19

D*allas in early August is a steam bath*, Mackenzie sighed. *Just two more weeks, then I'll be glad to get back home to Winston again. Still, it's good catching up Wendy.*

Her sister's life, Mackenzie realized, was far more hectic than her own schedule as a small town high school English teacher. It seemed like Wendy and her husband Bryan were always attending a conference or seminars, when they weren't involved with their busy social lives as university professors. Mackenzie wasn't used to the pace, and couldn't say that she liked it.

Morgan seemed to be enjoying herself, playing with her older cousin, Adam. A boy four years her senior, Adam indulged his cousin readily, and was quite protective of her.

But Mackenzie's heart ached when her daughter asked about Mick.

They had been in Dallas for two weeks, and Mackenzie's found her thoughts constantly turning to him. Those deep blue eyes; that wavy black hair; his smile that revealed perfect white teeth and that great big dimple in his cheek. She called him once, only to find the number to his land line disconnected. She did not bother calling his cell.

So, he left, huh? she fumed. *Bailed. Just like…* She tried to stop herself from going down that path, but the thoughts wouldn't be put on hold. *Sure, he was kind, and generous, and helpful. But in the end, he bailed on me and Morgan.*

But did he? The thought wouldn't leave her alone. *Wasn't it you that got cold feet and walked…no ran…away?*

Her argument with herself was interrupted by a tiny voice. "Mommy? Can we see Mick tomorrow?" Morgan was picking at her breakfast, looking a bit forlorn. Wendy and Darla paused over their coffee, exchanged those infuriating glances with each other, then stared directly at Mackenzie, waiting for her answer.

Mackenzie wanted to shake her finger at her mother and sister and tell them it was none of their business. Instead, she sipped her coffee, picked up the business section of the Dallas Morning News, and flipped through the pages.

"No, Baby," she answered. "Mick had to go away on a business trip." A picture caught her eye, and she let out a startled gasp.

"What is it, dear," Darla asked.

"Uh, nothing. Just a story in the paper." She glanced at Morgan before continuing, "There's a picture of… someone… shaking hands with someone else."

Wendy snatched the paper from her sister's hands.

"Lambert Group purchases Sweden-based Rieux Pharmaceuticals for $7 Billion Dollars," she read the headline out loud. "Someone said the Lambert Group acquired the pharmaceutical company because of its groundbreaking work in diabetes research. And Someone hopes to increase the amount of money dedicated to research and development of new drugs and protocols to combat diabetes."

Wendy folded the paper and handed it back to Mackenzie, looking very much like the cat who swallowed the canary. "Well, now we know where *Someone* ran off to," she grinned. "Pretty sure *Someone* didn't need to make a huge investment in a company that just happens to make diabetes treatments. I wonder what *Someone's* reasons were?"

Mackenzie swallowed, struggling to fight back the tears.

"Look Sis," Wendy reached across the table and patted her hand. "Don't you think you've had enough time to think? It's as plain as your curly red hair that the man loves you. If you can't see that…"

"He left," Mackenzie exploded. "Without a word, he just… left. What kind of love is that?"

"*He* left?" Her mother raised an eyebrow and let the question hang in the air. At last she continued. "You have the direct number to his New York office. You even have his personal cell phone number."

A tear rolled down Mackenzie's cheek. "Mom, I chased after Jared. We all know how that turned out. The days of me chasing after a man are over. If I'm worth having, I'm worth *being* chased."

CHAPTER 20

The first day of a new school year was always so exciting for Mackenzie; new students, new challenges, a new start. Perhaps the busyness of her schedule would help her forget Mick.

Nothing else has, she thought, a wry frown creasing her lips.

It had been a month since she climbed on the plane for Dallas, and she hadn't seen him, or heard from him, since. He was never far from her thoughts, though. It didn't help that Morgan asked about him every day.

Still, the school invigorated her. She loved the pale cream colors of the halls, the warm woods of the classroom doors, all the little touches that made the learning environment so inviting.

She allowed a smile to decorate her face as the children filed into the classroom. She felt good. *Well, maybe not good,* she thought, the smile fading as she reflected on her decreased energy level. She also pondered on her recent weight loss, and noticed her clothes not fitting as well as they used to. *That's what you get for falling in love.* She shook the thought from her mind, her red curls bouncing.

Mick pulled off his tie and dropped it on the couch as he stepped into his Manhattan apartment. He kicked off his shoes before heading into the kitchen and rummaging through the fridge for a bottle of orange juice. *What a month,* he mused.

Sweden, Germany, England, Canada…and that's not counting LA and Miami. Lambert Group keeps you busy if you let it.

Mick walked to the window that overlooked the skyline of the city that never sleeps, and wished he could shut out the world for a while. He had hoped throwing himself into the business would keep his thoughts at bay. *No such luck,* he thought, taking another swig of OJ. His thoughts continued to turn to the quiet, sleepy little community of Winston, Colorado, and two redheads who held his heart and mind captive. He glanced at his watch. *Six o'clock.* He did the calculation in his head. *Four o'clock in Colorado.* He pulled his cell phone from his pocket and hit the speed dial.

"Hello, this is John Austen speaking."

"Hello John. How are you today?" Mick turned away from the view of the city and plopped down on the couch.

"Hello, son. I'm doing great, how 'bout you?"

Mick could hear the squeak of the pastor's office chair as he pushed back.

"Ah, you know. Been better. Nothing your daughter couldn't fix. How is she?"

"I would say fine, but it wouldn't do for a preacher of the gospel to lie," John answered. "She's troubled. A blind man can see it. But she won't talk about it. At least, not to me."

"Yeah," Mick grumbled. "Not to me, either."

John tried to change the subject. "You've been busy lately. Your picture has been all over the newspapers and the evening news on TV. Seems like the Lambert Group has gone on a buying spree lately, snapping up lot of companies. That pharmaceutical company in Sweden; that wouldn't have anything to do with a little red haired girl, now, would it?"

Mick grinned. "The Lambert Group had been looking at

Rieux Pharmaceuticals for a long time. Trust me, as much as a little red haired girl has been on my mind, dropping $7 billion to buy a foreign company isn't something the board would approve just 'cause I wanted it. The fact that they are an industry leader in diabetes research is more of a happy happenstance."

"I know you have important work to do with The Lambert Group," John said, his mood turning somber. "But I'll tell you the truth; Darla and I miss you here. Morgan misses you. And I'm pretty sure Mackenzie does too. I'm just not sure she knows how to say it."

Mick nodded. "Tell her I said hi, okay? I'll call you next week. 'Bye, sir."

He looked out the window at the New York skyline. It was spectacular, no doubt about it. But it wasn't Winston, Colorado.

Mackenzie pushed the doorbell, and listened to the cheerful chime on the other side of the door. A moment later, Patty Reichart, Mackenzie's best friend from elementary school days, opened the door to the posh apartment.

"Hi, Mackenzie, come on in," Patty said, giving her friend a hug. "Hi Morgan, Jaime will be glad to see you."

Blonde, a little taller than Mackenzie and twenty pounds curvier, Patty worked the night shift as a Registered Nurse. She was also a single mom of a three-year-old. Mackenzie marveled at the spotless apartment. *How does she manage it, with no help at all? I can barely get Morgan dressed and to day care on time.*

"How about some tea? I've got Earl Grey and Raspberry Spice." Patty put the kettle on the stove and got down two delicate china cups.

"Morgan seems to be doing great with her diabetes," Patty observed. "She looks like she's putting on weight."

They sat at the kitchen table; Mackenzie placed her chin in her hand. "She's has gained four pounds. Dr. Brock is pleased with her progress."

Patty poured the water into the cups and sat back down. "You, on the other hand, don't look so great. How are you? You look like you've lost weight, and while I could certainly stand to drop a few pounds, you...not so much, girlfriend."

"I've just been busy at school and with Morgan," Mackenzie brushed the comment away while stirring her tea. "How about you? I don't see how you do it alone. Your place looks great."

"When the good Mr. Reichart decided to trade me in for a new model, I made sure he took care of Jaime's needs, and that includes having a cleaning service come once a week."

"So, that's your secret," Mackenzie laughed.

"No more rumors of me having super powers," Patty, chuckled as she sipped her tea.

"Mommy, Mommy," Jaime came running into the kitchen. "Morgan's sick!"

Both women leapt up and ran to the living room. Morgan lay on the floor on her back sweating profusely.

Patty kicked into nurse mode. "I'd say her blood sugar is low. Do you have her monitor with you?"

Mackenzie pulled the device from her pocket and handed it to her friend, who took a quick reading.

"Yeah, she's low, forty-six." Patty hurried to the kitchen, then came back with a small glass of milk and a cookie. "Sit her up. Here Morgan, drink this." She put the glass to her lips and encouraged her to take a big gulp. "Eat this, baby. It's good."

"Morgan's sick," Jaime kept repeating. She was obviously distraught over her friend's health.

"She'll be fine, Jaime," Patty soothed the child. "You'll see. Just give her a minute."

Before long Morgan was back to normal. Patty checked her blood sugar again. "Ninety-three," she announced. "It might spike a little high later. Check her before dinner anyway, in case she needs insulin."

Mackenzie made a big fuss over Jaime for alerting them. The children went back to playing dress-up, while the adults went back to their now tepid tea.

"I don't know, Patty. Sometimes she's fine and other times I can't get her to eat anything. I think she just really misses… Mick."

"Ah yes, the legend of the pediatrics ward," Patty allowed a wry smile to cross her face. "He has quite a reputation among the nurses. I never met him, but I heard kids idolized him. And according to Julie Watson, who knows a think or two about men, he is, and I quote, 'Fine! Umm, umm, umm!' Not to mention wealthy. Did you know The Lambert Group owns Winston General, along with a bunch of other hospitals all across the country?"

"No," Mackenzie grimaced over the lukewarm tea. "No I didn't."

Patty poured fresh, hot tea into their cups and the chatted for another thirty minutes.

"Thanks Patty, I should go," Mackenzie said at last. "It's been fun catching up. We should do it more often.

"Sounds great," Patty replied. "How 'bout we take in a movie Friday night? I know a couple of good sitters."

"You're on," Mackenzie said. *A night at the movies to get my mind off of…him…would be just the thing.* She gathered Morgan and headed for home.

John met her at the door. He picked Morgan up and swung her around before giving Mackenzie a kiss on the forehead. "Your Mom has a meeting with the school board, so I ordered a couple of pizzas for dinner. Hope that all right with you. I got pepperoni for Morgan and extra cheese for you."

"That's fine, dad," Mackenzie said.

"You okay? You look a bit flustered."

"Morgan had a low blood sugar spell at Patty's this afternoon," she sighed, her frustration overflowing. "Sometimes she won't eat, and well, you know." Mackenzie checked Morgan's blood sugar and shook her head. She administered a small bolus of insulin.

John said the prayer and reached for a slice of pizza. He paused for a moment before taking a bite, then decided to go through with it.

"He said to tell you hello." He bit into the pizza and chewed without looking at his daughter. He didn't need to see her to feel the temperature in the room drop.

"He said, 'hello.' You spoke to him, and he said, 'hello?' When? How long…" She was incredulous. "Why did you…" Her voice trailed off. She was afraid she would lose control if she said any more.

John stared at his pizza, wondering if there was any chance of chasing the worms back into the can he had opened. He tried to choose his words carefully.

"Baby, we've talked on the phone every week since he left Winston. Is that a problem for you?"

Her eyes flashed. "Yes, it's a problem! Whose side are you one, anyway?" She dropped her pizza onto her plate and glared at her father.

"Sweetheart, I'm on the side of doing what's right. To the best of my knowledge, he hasn't done anything wrong."

"He dumped us, Dad," she exploded. "I told him I needed time to think, and he just left. And you don't think he has done anything wrong?"

"Seems to me the one who did the dumping and just leaving…was you," John answered. Mackenzie's jaw dropped and stared at her father. "I'm the one who told him you needed time, that he should keep his distance and give you the space to sort things out, and that the real test of love was patience."

"You know I have a problem with trust, dad. That's one of the things I needed time to think about."

"And I'm pretty sure you wouldn't be able to think clearly if he were here, constantly distracting you with his presence. Am I right?"

Mackenzie pondered her father's wisdom for a moment before responding. Then nodded.

"I was afraid I was falling in love with him," she confessed, a tear starting to form in the corner of her eye. "Now I'm not so sure." John raised an eyebrow, but said nothing. "Honestly, I'm not sure about much of anything anymore, except that I have to take care of Morgan." She cast her eyes at her daughter, who was cheerfully munching on her slice of pepperoni pizza.

"You could call him…"

"Dad, thank you," Mackenzie cut him off. "I know you want to help. But I'm a big girl. I can deal with this on my own."

John nodded, and they ate the rest of their meal in silence.

Mackenzie cried herself to sleep that night.

CHAPTER 21

Mackenzie didn't feel like her old self Sunday morning. She had been tired and cranky all week, but when Sunday dawned she felt horrible. She had no energy and her stomach felt like it was tied in knots.

It's just nerves, she thought as she dropped Morgan at the nursery. Frustrated with her inability to overcome her own anxieties, Mackenzie turned to prayer. *Lord, please help me through this morning's service. I ask you to strengthen me. Flow through me. In Jesus name, amen.*

The musicians were already warming up as she entered the sanctuary. Church members were filtering in, choosing their favorite seats and catching up with each other. Mackenzie was surrounded by laughter and conversation. She tried to smile, but she simply didn't have the energy for it. She turned around and headed for the water fountain in the lobby. She was relieved to see her friend, Patty Reichart, walking out of the ladies' room. She made a beeline for her.

"Patty! I'm so glad to see you." She pulled her friend aside.

Patty squeezed her friend's hand. "You look terrible. What's wrong?"

"I don't know," Mackenzie confessed. "I'm tired all the time. My stomach hurts. I can't seem to get enough to drink and I'm constantly having to go to the bathroom."

Patty placed the back of her hand on Mackenzie's forehead,

then on her neck. "You don't seem to have a temperature, but..." her voice trailed off as a look of concern crossed her eyes. "I think we need to get you to the ER." Patty started to get up, but Mackenzie pulled her back down.

"I can't, I'm singing this morning."

"I don't think so," her friend answered in her authoritative *Nurse Patty* voice. "Stay right here."

"But what about Morgan?" Mackenzie started to stand.

"I'll take care of it," Patty answered. "Sit!"

Mackenzie didn't have the strength to argue. "I'm going to be sick." Patty helped her to the ladies' room, then held onto her and wiped her face with a damp paper towel. "What is wrong with me?" Mackenzie asked, her voice shaking.

"Do you have Morgan's monitor with you?"

"No, I don't usually bring it to church because we go home right after...," she sucked in a deep breath as they left the building. "Are you thinking what I think your thinking?"

"I can't be sure, Honey, but you have all the symptoms. I've called your mom. She'll take care of Morgan. You need to come with me, now."

Patty helped her to climb into her SUV and started toward the hospital. Mackenzie moaned and settled back into the seat.

"I'm thirsty. I'm so thirsty."

"Hang on, we're almost there."

Mackenzie closed her eyes, her thoughts drifting to the last time she went to the ER... with Mick. She heard voices calling her name; people saying things she did not understand. She felt a warmth wash over her, and a strange sense of peace. It felt so good to rest.

She found it impossible to move. She tried to open her eyes, but the effort was too much. She heard a familiar voice calling out from a distance. *Sing… sing… sing Mackenzie; sing for me. It was like a low, sweet whisper in her ear. Sing for me, Mackenzie. Do not be afraid. Do not be afraid for your child. You are not alone I am with you. I have a plan for you. When you look around you, you will see. Sing of love, sing of love sing, Mackenzie.* Then it was gone and she sank into oblivion.

The sound of voices and the rattle of a cart being pushed in the distance roused her from sleep. Mackenzie opened her eyes. Confusion clouded her mind. Monitors beeped softly behind her. Her hand was tethered to a plastic tube and a nurse was hanging a bag of clear liquid on a hook above her head.

"Where am I," Mackenzie whispered.

"Oh, good," the nurse said with a cheerful smile. "You're awake. How do you feel?"

Mackenzie had to think about that for a moment.

"I…um. I think I feel okay. What am I…I mean…" Mackenzie's eyes suddenly flew wide open and tried to sit up. "Where's my daughter? Where's Morgan?"

The nurse pressed her back down, and calmed her.

"Your daughter's fine," the nurse reassured her. "She's with your parents. I'll let the doctor know you are awake, and he'll be in after awhile. You're in the intensive care unit at Winston General Hospital."

"Intensive care?"

"You had a pretty rough go of it, young lady," the nurse answered. "You were unconscious when you arrived at the ER three days ago."

"Three days?" Mackenzie was still trying to understand what was going on.

"Good thing for you your friend is a nurse. Things could have gone south real fast. Now, I need to check your blood sugar."

Mackenzie knew the routine from Morgan. While the nurse performed her duties, Mackenzie looked around the room. It was filled with flowers; roses, daisies, bouquets of every imaginable sort in vases and baskets.

"You have a lot of friends," the nurse smiled. "And your Mr. Lambert is so sweet. He calls at least once every day. Sometimes two or three times."

Mackenzie's heart leapt. "Mr. Lambert…called?"

"Um hm. Do you feel up to talking next time he calls?"

Yes! she wanted to scream. But she could only manage a hoarse, "Yes, please."

The nurse nodded, finished her duties, then left just as a pair of figures in white lab coats entered. "Good morning, Mackenzie," said Dr. Vogan, Mackenzie's family doctor. An older woman with a quick wit and a mischievous grin, Dr. Vogan flipping open a chart and made a quick appraisal. "I'm glad to see you awake. This is Dr. Meyers, he admitted you."

"Dr. Vogan, I'm glad to see you. What happened to me?"

"Well," she said peering over the top of her glasses, "It appears you slipped into unconsciousness during your ride to the ER. Your glucose readings were extremely high and you were in ketoacidosis. I'm sure you can fill in the blanks since you've already been through this with Morgan. We'll be taking you up to a room in a little bit. When we get you regulated, you can go home. Questions?"

She looked from one doctor to the other. "How long will that take?"

"That depends. Maybe a week, maybe a few days longer."

"So, I'm diabetic?" Mackenzie groaned.

"I'm afraid so," Dr. Vogan answered.

Mackenzie nodded as all the information clicked into place.

The tiredness, the incessant thirst; it all made sense now. "May I see Morgan?"

Dr. Vogan smiled at her, "I'll see what I can do. I'll try to check on you this afternoon if I have the chance."

Later that morning Mackenzie was moved from ICU to a regular hospital room on the fifth floor. A kind-faced nurse helped her shower and wash her hair. She was just settling in for lunch when there came a knock on her door and Patty came in.

"My hero," Mackenzie exclaimed. "Am I glad to see you." Tears rolled down her cheeks as Patty hugged her.

"Hey, take it easy. You're going to get your lunch wet." Patty grabbed a box of tissues from the counter and handed one to her friend. "Here. I'm glad you finally came around. Sorry I can't stay and chat, but I'm on duty. I just wanted to check in make sure they're taking good care of you." They hugged, Patty left and Mackenzie finished her lunch.

The afternoon was filled with blood glucose monitoring, vital readings and worry. *Worry? I don't have time to worry. I have a daughter to raise, a job to do and things that need my attention. Those seem like pretty good reasons to worry. But God said he would supply all my needs.*

She closed her eyes and started to pray when that same low, sweet whisper tickled her thoughts; Sing!

And she did. With her eyes closed and her voice low, Mackenzie worshipped in song, then fell into a deep, peaceful asleep.

The incessant ringing beside her bed jarred her from her sleep. She stared at the desk telephone as if it were a relic from the far distant past. I guess hospitals still have landlines. She giggled a bit at the thought.

"Hello," she croaked into the receiver.

"Hi Mac. I'm so glad to hear your voice."

"Mick?" She thought her heart may have skipped a beat. "Mick is that you?"

"In the flesh. Well, not really in the flesh, but at least in the spirit," Mick joked. "I would be there in the flesh, but I'm in South America, and…well, the truth is…I wasn't really sure if you wanted to see me…I mean, in the flesh."

She melted at the warmth in his voice. *Don't do that, he'll only let you and Morgan down.*

"I have missed you Mac; you and Morgan. Do you need anything? Can I do anything for you?"

She wanted to tell him, *Just love me. Just be there for me and my daughter. Just never leave us.* Instead she said, "I haven't seen Morgan since I was was admitted. But you can't do anything about that." Her voice carried the frustration she felt, "They won't let her in to see me."

"Maybe I can talk them into it," Mick said. "In the words of the wise Morgan, *You've got it, Baby!*"

"Mick, not even you can get her in to see me. But it's sweet of you to offer."

"Mackenzie, my phone is about to die. I'm hopping the next plane out. I will be there before long. Take care. I'm praying for you. 'Bye."

Mackenzie hung up the phone. and a tear rolled down her cheek.

CHAPTER 22

I *must belong to the prayingest church in the whole state,* Mackenzie thought, after receiving a multitude of visits, phone calls, cards and flowers from friends and church members. But her heart nearly cracked wide open when the florist delivered four dozen roses – forty-seven white, and one single red rose.

Lovely! she thought as she retrieved the card that came with them.

They pale in comparison to you. You've got it, Baby!

Mick

Mackenzie was wiping away tears when the door opened and her father entered, carrying Morgan.

"Mommy, Mommy!" Morgan held out her arms for Mackenzie. "Missed you so big, Mommy."

The child grabbed Mackenzie's face, pulled it close and kissed her on the forehead. Mackenzie hugged her tight and kissed her back.

"I missed you so big, too," she said. "Hi Dad, how did you manage to smuggle Morgan in here?"

"Dr. Vogan called your mother and told her to bring her up. Your mother's at the nurses' station talking to Patty. I'm so thankful to see you out of intensive care. You look much better." He bent down and placed a kiss on her cheek.

"Mommy sick," Morgan asked.

"Mommy has diabetes, Baby. Just like you." Mackenzie smiled.

"Mommy brave, just like me?"

Mackenzie smiled. "I try, Baby."

"How brave?" Morgan giggled and placed her thumb and forefinger close together.

Mackenzie laughed and put her palms a foot apart, "About this brave. I'm not as brave as you are yet." Darla Austen came into the room, hugged and kissed Mackenzie, then sat down next to her husband.

"Well Mackenzie, it seems you have a guardian angel looking after you," Darla smiled.

"Yes, I know."

"In more ways than one, dear," her mother had that infuriating smug look that said, *I know something you don't know.*

"Okay, spill it," Mackenzie insisted. "What is it you are intentionally *not* saying."

Darla laughed and clapped her hands. "Patty just told me that *Mr. Lambert* is the one who is responsible for Morgan being here today."

"Mr. Lambert, huh?" Mackenzie repeated, a wry smile twisting her lips. "And just how did he do that?"

"It seems he's on a first name basis with the hospital administrator; old golfing buddies, or something like that"

Her father smiled. "It doesn't hurt that the Lambert Group owns this hospital. I'd say if Mick Lambert wants a little special attention, and it doesn't compromise patient welfare, he's probably going to get whatever he asks for."

"Oh my word!" Mackenzie hugged Morgan again. "I owe him big time."

"You'll have the opportunity to thank him in person. He's on his way, you know, flying in from South America. He was in the middle of some big business deal, but he turned it over to

one of his associates and caught the last plane out last night."
Her Dad winked at her.

"You talked with him?"

"We talk frequently, Baby. He is a good man."

"But…he walked away from us," Mackenzie said, her voice
barely audible.

"Maybe. Maybe not," her father answered.

CHAPTER 23

Mick Lambert tossed his duffel bag into the back of the Jeep and hopped into the passenger seat. They lurched away from the mining camp and headed toward the small village where his Cessna Turbo Skylane single prop airplane waited to fly him to Ecuador's Cotopaxi International Airport.

Then what, he wondered.

A connecting flight in Dallas or on to Atlanta? Atlanta's the wrong direction, but that's where the company jet is. The private jet will get me to Winston faster than trying to make connecting flights out of Dallas.

Atlanta it is.

CHAPTER 24

Mackenzie placed her Bible on the stand beside her bed. She closed her eyes and leaned back to pray. "Lord, was that your voice telling me to sing? I don't understand. I do sing for you - at Winston Faith Center. What do you mean?"

She opened her eyes and looked through the window at the setting sun that was streaking the sky with deep purples and pinks.

So beautiful, Mackenzie thought.

As natural as breathing, she opened her mouth and sang, "Jesus my Rock... My Rock, My Sword, My Shield."

Patty stood outside her room listening, a blissful smile creasing her face. Once the singing stopped, she wiped away a tear, then knocked and entered the room. "Hey Girl, I'm heading out and wanted to check on you. How're you doing?"

"I'm fine; just been praying." Mackenzie patted the side of the bed and Patty sat down.

"Has Dr. Vogan said when you might get to go home?"

"No, not yet," Mackenzie pouted. "She said, 'we'll talk about it tomorrow.' I can't tell you how much I appreciate everything you've done, Patty." She squeezed her friend's hand.

"Well, when you get home we'll have to take in that movie. As I recall we were supposed to have already gone, but someone went and got herself thrown in the hospital."

Mackenzie laughed. "Hug Jaime for me," she said.

"I will. Get some rest. I'll see you in the morning."

The sun disappeared behind the mountains, and Mackenzie allowed herself to drift into a peace-filled sleep, disturbed routinely by nurses taking her vital signs or checking her blood glucose level.

Morning brought the welcome news that if things continued to progress, she could go home day after tomorrow. She showered and changed into a fresh gown. Dr. Vogan suggested the possibility of an insulin pump and scheduled a meeting for her with a company representative. The thought appealed to her.

Modern technology, she mused. *What will they think of next?*

A sharp rap on the door snapped her out of her thoughts and a familiar voice called out, "Mackenzie?"

"Mick?" Her heart raced.

CHAPTER 25

Mick peeked inside the room, then walked to her side, the look of sincere affection beaming from his face. He bent over her and kissed her cheek. "I've missed you, Mac."

"I've missed you, too," Mackenzie whispered, trying to keep her emotions in check, but failing miserably. After a moment the dam burst and and the tears flowed freely down her cheeks.

"Why did you go away," she demanded. She searched his eyes, trying to read him.

Mick was dumbfounded. He held up a finger to signal a pause in the conversation, then pulled a chair up next to her bed and sat down.

"You said you needed time," he explained. "I thought I was respecting your wishes."

Exasperation filled her voice. "I never said I wanted you to go away. The truth is, Mick I have a real problem trusting men. After what happened with Jared…"

"I'm not Jared."

"But you left," she accused. "As soon as we came home from Wendy's, I drove out to your house and you were just gone - packed up and gone."

"I did go away," Mick admitted, "but I did not pack up."

"The 'For Sale' sign was gone."

"Of course it was gone, Mac. Because I bought the house."

"You…bought the house?" Her voice trailed off.

"I told you when we first started dating that I had an option to buy the place." Mick explained. "You said you needed time, and then you left town - without so much as a goodbye, I might add – so I figured it would be a good time for me to take care of some business while giving you the space you needed."

"Oh," Mackenzie's voice felt small and more than a bit fragile. "Did you…" she bit her lip, then continued. "Did you buy that pharmaceutical company because of Morgan?"

Mick just smiled. "I thought it would be a good investment. The company is doing a lot of fantastic work on diabetes research. They've made a lot of advances, particularly with insulin pumps."

Mackenzie looked at him without saying anything for a moment. "Mick, I need to apologize, for what I've said and what I've thought. And I want to thank you for all that you have done. Thank you for getting Morgan in to see me. Can you forgive me?"

He mimicked her trademark head tilt and smiled. "How can I not? Isn't that what a knight would do?"

"Yes, of course, sir," Mackenzie giggled. "By the way, how is Gringolet?"

"What is it that Batman says? 'Chicks dig the car.' Gringolet is just fine, right where I left her in the garage. I'm sure she'll be glad to see you again."

She took a deep breath, then blew it out. She gazed into his eyes with a touch of sadness in her own. "Mick, I want you to know that I like you; I like you very much. But I'm still not ready to commit to…well, to anything yet. I don't want you to leave. But I need time to work through some things. Can you understand?"

With those soft green eyes burning into his soul, she could

have asked him for anything, and he would do it. He took her hand and brushed it with a kiss.

"Of course," was all he said.

CHAPTER 26

The two weeks following Mackenzie's release from the hospital flew by. She worked hard to adjust to the insulin pump. The new exercise regimen took some getting used to, but she was determined to embrace her new lifestyle. Her family and friends provided a constant flow of encouragement, and of course there was Morgan to keep her life interesting.

I honestly don't have much to complain about, she thought as she placed Morgan in her car seat. Her reverie was interrupted by the buzz of her cell phone.

"Hello?"

"Hi Mackenzie," Patty's voice came over the phone, "Hey, I won't keep you. I know you're leaving work right about now. I want to ask you if it would be okay if I bring a friend to dinner tomorrow?"

Mackenzie laughed, thrilled that her friend may have finally found a guy who made her happy.

"It's okay with me," she said. "But it's really Mick's dinner party. He's the one who arranged everything. You, me, the parents *and the kids* at Winston's most exclusive restaurant? Only a man would make those arrangements."

"Well, it does have that classy grand piano, and a guy playing jazz while you eat. What's not to love," Patty countered. "I mean, except for the kids sword fighting with the bread sticks."

"So, who's the friend you're bringing to dinner? Anyone I know?"

There was a pregnant pause on the line that made Mackenzie wonder if her cell phone had dropped the call.

"Patty?"

"Yeah, I'm here." Patty answered. "And yeah, you know him. It's Robert Mann. You remember him? Mick's friend?"

"Robert Mann, the record producer?" Mackenzie's jaw dropped. "Um, yeah, I remember him. Really nice guy. But, how…I mean, where did…?" She fumbled her words as she slid behind the wheel of her compact and started the car.

"He was with Mick at the hospital one day. We visited while Mick was with you. He said he was in town looking for office space, that he really fell in love with the area the last time he was in town and…Anyway, we've gone out a few times, and… Do you mind? Please tell me you don't mind. I really like him, and…"

"Of course I don't mind," Mackenzie shook her head. "You deserve a great guy in your life, and if Robert makes you happy, then I'm thrilled for you."

"Thanks Mac, you're the best. I just didn't want things to get…awkward…know what I mean?"

Oh, I know all about things getting awkward, Mackenzie thought. Aloud she said, "No problem. Sounds like it's going to be a fun evening."

Patty giggled like a school girl on the night before prom. "I hope I have something appropriate to wear. The restaurant is out of my price range, so I've never been. I just don't want to be underdressed."

"Hey, take it easy," Mackenzie laughed. "It isn't black tie and tails. Romano's might be the most exclusive joint in Winston, but this is still Winston."

"I know," Patty answered. "It's just that, I really, *really* like

Robert and I don't want to come across as some hick from the sticks."

Mackenzie checked the traffic and turned right onto the street. "Just be yourself," she advised her friend. "Gotta go. Not supposed to be on the cell while I'm driving."

Mackenzie punched the disconnect button and drove the rest of the way to school in silence. She had not known Robert Mann was in town, and wasn't sure how she felt about it. She had to admit she had thought about his offer from time to time. *And that voice at the hospital. Was that just a fantasy due to the medication, or was God actually trying to tell me something? If there was ever a time to pray, this is it.* "Seriously God," she prayed out loud. "You've got my attention. I'm listening. Talk to me. Please!"

She cocked her head and listened, but heard no sound except her daughter's voice, singing joyfully in the car seat behind her.

CHAPTER 27

Mackenzie helped her mother with dinner than night, as usual. She was intent on slicing tomatoes, when a familiar tune caught her ear.

"What is that you're humming, Mom?"

Darla reached into the oven to check on the roast. "Something I heard on the radio this morning; 'Just One of Those Things.' I really like that song."

"Yeah, it's a catchy tune. I've just never heard you sing much secular music."

"Well, I suppose there's nothing wrong with a good love song, especially when you're in love. Don't you agree?" Her mother winked at her as she added some sugar to the pitcher of iced tea. Her recent visit to Texas had given her a new appreciation for the Southern delicacy of 'sweet tea.'

"I appreciate a good love song as much as the next girl," Mackenzie countered. "But you and Dad never even allowed me to listen to secular music when I was growing up."

"Well, times change," was all her mother said. She smiled and went about setting the table.

After a pleasant, if uneventful, supper, Mackenzie spent the night grading papers, reading her Bible and praying.

Lord, I could really use a word from you right about now. What do I do about Mick? I like him. I really do. I think I might even love him. But I can't love him. Love means trust, and I'm just not sure I know how to trust any man right now. A still small voice seemed to whisper, *You trust your father. He's a man.*

That's not the same thing; not the same thing at all! Mackenzie shook her head, her red curls slapping against her cheeks. *Mick is not my father. He's just a friend; a good friend; but he wants to be more and I don't know how to be more for him. I know. I know. Morgan needs a father, and Mick adores her. He would be such a great father, but…*

But what? the small voice asked.

I don't know, but what? she whispered aloud. Tears clouded her vision. She buried her face in her pillow and cried herself to sleep.

The days leading up to the big dinner party strolled by, as if there was nothing to be in a hurry about. Mackenzie found herself looking forward to the evening. She needed a chance to relax and enjoy herself. She hurried home after school dismissed and immediately started preparing for the evening. First she drew a nice, hot bubble bath. She couldn't remember the last time she had indulged in such a girly luxury. She giggled to herself. *What were the lyrics to the song, 'I Enjoy Being a Girl'?*

Mackenzie fluffed and primped and changed her dress three times before finally deciding on a demure, but figure hugging, deep green sheath dress that perfectly accented her red hair. At 6:30 sharp the doorbell rang. Her heart raced. She took one last look in the mirror, patted her hair to make sure everything was in place, and sashayed over to the front door.

There he was with his dimpled smile, looking for all the world like a modern-day knight in shining armor.

"Hi Mick, don't you look charming this evening."

"Hey, that's my job; that, and to tell you how gorgeous you

are. Is that a new dress? I haven't seen it before. You look… amazing!" He admired the way the simple green dress accented her figure without revealing an inch of skin. And the way her hair cascaded in curls to her shoulders was the perfect frame for her lovely face. He couldn't resist. He gave her a quick hug and a peck on the lips.

"Mmm," he grinned, licking his lips. "Is your blood sugar high today, or are you always just naturally sweet?"

"Mick. Mick. Hi, Mick!" Morgan ran up to him, her arms outstretched. He snatched her up in his arms.

"Hi, Baby. How's my girl?"

"Okay, Mick. Jaime coming?"

"Jaime will meet us there. Where are your grandparents?"

"Right here," Darla called from the hallway. "It was nice of you to offer to drive us. I didn't hear anything so you must have left *the beast* at home."

"You're safe, at least for the time being," Mick laughed. "I brought the Mercedes. We couldn't all fit into Gringolet, but I'll take you for a ride in her one day. I think you'll like it."

"I don't know about that," Darla wrinkled her nose. "I'm sure it would deafen me."

"No, it wouldn't Mom. It's really fun." Mackenzie smiled at Mick as he hooked Morgan's car seat into place in the rear. John and Darla climbed in on either side of the child and Mick walked around to the passenger side to open the door for Mackenzie.

"It's such a beautiful evening. Can we open the roof, please," she asked. A hint of early autumn brushed the leaves with color and the sunset was spectacular. Mick touched a button on the dash and the sunroof slid open.

"This is a nice feature," Darla said. "John, next time we buy a car, we should make sure it has a sunroof."

"Careful what you wish for, mom," Mackenzie snickered. "It's a slippery slope. First you want a sunroof; next you'll want a convertible. Before you know it, you're hooked and you'll be driving down the highway in a vintage roadster with loud, noisy side pipes!"

Darla was still protesting as they wheeled into the parking lot of Romano's Restaurant. Mick pulled up to the door and got out allowing the valet to take the car.

The maitre d' escorted them to their table. Rob, Patty and Jaime were already waiting.

"This is some place," Patty laughed. "Quite different from the hospital cafeteria."

Mackenzie opened her clutch and took out the meter that communicated with her pump. Patty knew what her best friend was doing and commented, "Mick that was a fantastic investment you made in Rieux. Only a few years ago she would not have been able to do that."

"Do what," Rob asked.

Patty explained the process as Mackenzie entered the carbohydrate count for her meal into the meter. The device would then automatically factor in the appropriate insulin dosage and, with the touch of a finger, trigger the pump to deliver it.

Mackenzie put the meter back in her purse. "Maybe someday they will figure out how to get them to work on two-year-olds."

"Yes, your company is making tremendous progress," Darla added. "Thank you, Mick."

"Don't thank me, Darla. All I did was buy it." Mick grinned.

Mackenzie was having a great time. She was relaxed and talked at ease with her friends and family. When the waiter brought their menus, Mackenzie was surprised and delighted to find plenty of tempting dishes that would fit her diet as well as Morgan's. Once they ordered, she and Patty excused themselves to the ladies room.

"So how are things progressing between you and Rob," Mackenzie pressed. "Come on. Spill."

Patty just grinned, "I think your rich boyfriend has very good taste in friends."

"He's...not really my boyfriend," Mackenzie backpedaled. "He's more of just...a friend."

"Uh huh," Patty replied as they made their way back to the table.

Their thoughtful waitress brought crayons and coloring sheets to help keep the children occupied while the adults engaged in pleasant small talk. The pianist played tasteful jazz and light contemporary music, occasionally singing along.

He's quite good, Mackenzie thought.

Their salads arrived and John Austen offered a quick blessing. Mackenzie had just taken a big bite of her salad when Rob suddenly turned to her and asked, "So, are you ready to sign with me yet?"

Mackenzie hid her surprise well, but she did manage to shoot Mick an accusatory glance. She swallowed, took a sip of water and dabbed the corners of her mouth with her napkin before answering.

She cocked her head, causing her curls to bounce around her shoulders – and Mick's heart to flipflop in his chest - and looked straight at Rob. "I'm still praying about it," she smiled. "I think I still need a little more time."

If Rob felt the heat in her voice, he didn't show it. "No worries," he said. "I just wanted you to know the offer is still on the table." Rob turned his attention back to his date and they all finished their meal in a relaxed, unhurried atmosphere, topping the evening off with coffee and Romano's trademark chocolate almond cheesecake.

"The food here is excellent," Mick said. "And this evening's company is superb." He turned his head toward Mackenzie and smiled. She could feel her heart creeping up into her throat.

An elderly gentleman three tables over made his way to the pianist and whispered a request. "I know the melody," the pianist told him, "but I'm afraid I don't know the lyrics."

The old man's face fell. "It's our 65th wedding anniversary tonight," he said. "That was the song we danced to the night we got married."

The pianist nodded, stopped playing, and leaned into his microphone. "Folks, we have a very special request tonight. Does anyone here happen to know the lyrics to *Young at Heart?*"

Diners looked around at each other, but no one raised a hand. Mackenzie knew the song. She raised her hand.

The pianist ran his fingers over the keyboard. "Excellent! Hey, I know you. You're Mackenzie Austen. I've heard you sing at church. I wouldn't normally ask, but it's this couple's 65th wedding anniversary. Could we get you to come up here and sing it for them? I know they would appreciate it. How 'bout it, folks? Can we give Mackenzie a hand?"

The dining room erupted in applause. Mackenzie looked at the faces around her table. Her father smiled and nodded at her. Mick squeezed her hand. "Knock 'em dead, Mac," he whispered close to her ear.

Mackenzie took a deep breath and stood. It wasn't that she was afraid of singing in public, but she felt a little blindsided by the request. She made her way to the piano, picked up the microphone and smiled at the elderly couple.

"This is a lovely song," she said. "Perfect for a young couple just starting out, such as yourselves."

She nodded to the pianist. He began playing; Mackenzie closed her eyes and let the music wash through her. She sang, her voice clear as crystal. When she opened her eyes, the anniversary couple were slow dancing in the middle of the floor. She sang to them, but she also held the other occupants of the room in her hands; diners stopped eating, servers stood mesmerized. She poured herself into the song, and when it was over the room exploded into applause and shouts of "More! More! Encore."

Mackenzie bowed to the audience and blew a kiss to the elderly couple who were moving back to their table. She leaned toward the pianist and whispered her own request. He grinned and started playing another familiar melody.

Mackenzie pointed to Morgan and sang, I've Got a Crush on You! Morgan clapped and giggled. Couples from around the room got up and danced. Mackenzie found herself exhilarated by the experience. The song ended and once more thunderous applause erupted.

"One more?" Mackenzie smiled into the microphone. The diners responded with shouts, claps and whistles.

"Okay. Let's kick it up a bit. This one's for you, Mom," she said, then launched into *It Was Just One of Those Things*. She moved to the rhythm of the music, swaying in time with the beat. Her energy was infectious. She owned the room.

The song ended with more applause. She held up her hand palm out, "Thank you." The diners stood and applauded as Mackenzie handed the microphone back to the awestruck pianist. She sashayed back to her table and sat down. She took a long sip of her iced tea, then turned toward Rob.

"Mr. Mann, I think I would like to sign your contract."

Rob's mouth dropped open in shock, and his eyes flew

wide, as if he had been hit in the head with a two-by-four. It only took a moment for him to regain his composure. "Absolutely," he answered. "By all means. Yes! How about Monday? You can come to my office, and bring your attorney, of course. I know you want to do exclusively Christian music, but after what I've just heard tonight, you should really consider expanding your options. Just think about it, please? Maybe pray about it?"

"Thank you, Rob," she said. "Okay, Monday after school it is. If it's okay with you, just let Mick look over the contract. If it's good enough for him, then it's good enough for me. I trust his business expertise." *Did I say I trust Mick? Where did that come from?* "The secular music part... I don't know. I just know that I loved singing just now. It made me feel good, like it does when I sing at church. I know God wants me to sing for Him but..."

Her Father broke in, "I think it would be wrong if it takes you away from God. To sing some secular songs, well, your mother and I like some of it. You need to follow your heart, but first and foremost you need to follow the Lord."

"Mackenzie, Solar Music has both Christian and general market labels," Rob said. "Believe me, I know the music industry can be a pretty dark place. But I am a believer, and I have no desire to see any of our artists move down an unhealthy path. I think what is important is that you pray about it and decide for yourself what you think God wants you to do. Which ever way you decide, Solar is behind you, 100 percent."

A short man with a big mustache and a round stomach came over to their table. "Good evening, I am Franco Romano. May we get you anything else? Please, your meal is on the house. We have never heard such singing. I should pay you, little lady." He motioned to the waitress. "More refills and deserts for these people."

Mackenzie lightly touched his arm. "On one condition, Mr. Romano," she smiled at him. "May I do one more song?"

"Ah, Grazie, you can sing here anytime, anytime!"

Patty smiled at her friend. "I think we've created a monster. What are you going to sing?"

"Request?" she looked around the table.

Mick cleared his throat, "How about, *All or Nothing at All*?"

Mackenzie rose and grinned at him. "You got it, Baby." The room grew quiet as she strode to the piano and picked up the microphone. She closed her eyes and possessed the song. When it was over, her heart felt light. She remembered a scene from the old movie, *Chariots of Fire*, and paraphrased a quote from Eric Liddle; *When I sing, I feel His pleasure!* She handed the microphone back to the pianist, smiled, and nodded to the applauding diners.

The ride home was fantastic. Mackenzie was elated and it showed. "Mick, would you mind going to practice with me tomorrow? I'll fix lunch for you."

"Practice? Oh, you mean for Sunday. I would love to, but why don't you let me order pizza. You can have pizza can't you? A little salad, diet coke, I can order for the band."

"Sure, that would be great! I... I would like to get your input on the contract with Rob... if you don't mind."

"Not at all. What time should I pick you up," he asked as he wheeled into the driveway.

"Eleven-ish?" Mackenzie said. Mick opened the door for Darla and helped her out of the car while John worked quietly to lift the sleeping Morgan from her car seat.

"Eleven-ish it is," Mick grinned. "I'll see you tomorrow. Try to get some rest. And Mac, you were really great tonight."

Mackenzie waited awkwardly as her parents stood on the steps in front of their door. Darla tapped her husband on the shoulder and nodded toward the inside. John finally took the hint and the older couple took the sleeping toddler inside the house, leaving Mackenzie and Mick to themselves for a moment.

As soon as the door closed Mackenzie threw her arms around Mick's neck and went up on tiptoes. She kissed him softly. When he pulled her into his embrace, she deepened the kiss. Her knees quivered. Breaking the moment, she whispered, "When I can say it without doubt, without fear, then I will say, I love you." She cocked her head and smiled into his face. "I won't do that until then, Mr. Michael David Lambert IV. But I will when the Lord opens the door for me."

"I can wait," he breathed into her hair. "I'm not going anywhere, Mac." He paused for a moment, enjoying the warmth of her body against his, then sighed. "Except home. See you tomorrow."

He kissed her hand and went to his car. Once on the street his mind went into autopilot. He prayed as if talking to an old and trusted friend. *I don't know, Lord. I've never been in love before. I can sort of understand her fear. No. That's a lie. I don't understand it at all. I mean, seriously God, I want to take care of her and Morgan. How is that a bad thing? She's not listening to me, but maybe she'll listen to you. How 'bout You tell her I'm a good guy? Man, God, you really gave that girl some talent. If the angels in heaven sing better than that, well…nah. I'm pretty sure that's not possible.*

Mackenzie slipped into her gown and picked up her Bible.

She plopped onto her bed and tried to read it, but she found herself going over the same passage again and again without really absorbing any of the words. At last she tossed the Bible aside and turned off the light.

She tried to pray, but the only words that came out were "Thank you. Thank you, Lord." She figured that was enough.

CHAPTER 28

It was 10:30 when Mick pulled into the Austen's driveway. It was a gorgeous blue jeans and T-shirt kind of day, and Mick was happy to oblige. He could do the three-piece-suit thing with the best of them, but he was most comfortable in a pair of worn Levi's and old sneakers. He shut off the engine and dropped his sunglasses into his shirt pocket before mounting the steps to the porch. The door opened before he could knock.

"I knew it was you when the pictures on the wall started rattling. Come on in." Darla Austen smiled broadly. "She's in the kitchen with Morgan."

"Mick," Morgan ran to him. "Pick me up!"

Mick gathered the toddler into his arms and snuggled her. "How's my girl?"

"I'm 'kay. How 'bout you, Mick?"

Mick noticed she was speaking in full sentences now. *Wow, they really do grow up fast,* he thought.

"I'm just fine, baby." He gave her a quick kiss on the cheek and set her down as Mackenzie entered the room. "Hi Mac."

"Coffee?" she smiled. She had pulled her hair back into a sloppy ponytail, and wore skinny jeans topped by a light green blouse which perfectly accented her red hair and made her eyes pop like sunlight.

"No thanks. I'm coffeed out."

"Patty called," Mackenzie said as she leaned against the

counter and sipped her coffee. "She plans to come to practice this morning."

"Really," Mick replied. "I didn't know she was in the choir. I didn't even know she sang."

"She isn't, and she doesn't," Mackenzie grinned. "I think she thinks a certain friend of yours might be there and, well…"

It was Mick's turn to grin. "Yeah, Rob has kept me up to date on that topic. He's pretty smitten himself, and I think Patty is good for him."

They said goodbye to Morgan and Darla, then headed for the car.

"Hello, Gringolet. It's been a while. How are you?"

Mick knitted his brows together and smirked. "Since when do you talk to cars?" He opened the door for her.

"Doesn't everybody?" She laughed as he got behind the wheel.

"Not really. Not unless she's giving me trouble. Then I talk to her, but you probably wouldn't want to hear what I say." He started the engine and pushed the gear shift into reverse. Smiling at her he said, "I admit I've found myself calling her Gringolet. I wonder why?" He dropped it into first gear and eased out the clutch. Straightening the wheel, he cracked the accelerator. The side pipes bellowed as the rear tires spun in a cloud of smoke. He grinned like a mischievous teenager and said, "Just a little something for your mother to enjoy."

The sounds of the musicians tuning up greeted them as they pulled up outside the sanctuary. Patty met them in the parking lot and rushed over for a hug.

"Hey Mac! How's the recording star?"

"Not so fast, Patty," she laughed. "You actually have to record a song before you can be called a 'recording star.' But thanks for the vote of confidence." She waved her hand in the air and laughed. The band members thronged her with questions. Apparently, the news of her impending recording contract was already common knowledge.

Mick was thrilled at the commotion. Mackenzie was in her element, and he loved seeing her happy. He pulled his cell phone from his pocket and punched in the number to the pizza parlor. He figured the least he could do right now was spring for lunch.

Patty sat down next to Mick as Mackenzie and the band took the platform. If she was disappointed that Rob hadn't shown up, she didn't show it. The band rehearsed a mix of songs ranging from slow, reverential worship numbers to bouncy, high energy praise songs. Mackenzie looked like she belonged there, like she owned the stage.

Once the pizzas arrived Mackenzie called for a break. Everyone headed for the fellowship hall, laughing and joking, with a bit of good-natured jostling for position to see who got the first slice. They gathered around the tables and talked about music, the church, the school and life in general. The conversation took Mick's thought down a road they hadn't traveled before.

I wonder if Mackenzie will keep teaching once her CD comes out? I wonder how she'll feel if she can't teach. I know how much she loves it; how fulfilling it is for her. Oh, well, God's got this. He's brought us this far. We'll figure it out as we go along.

He turned his attention back to the pizza, and to the redhead seated across the table from him.

CHAPTER 29

Robert Mann's office at Solar Music was on the fifteenth floor of the tallest building in Winston – the 1st National Bank Building, which had exactly fifteen floors. The view of the quaint little town surrounded by the mountains in the background was breathtaking. Mackenzie and Mick sat in dark blue leather chairs in front of the polished mahogany desk.

"I think you will find this contract to be fair. I have made flexibility arrangements so you may have time with Morgan and of course time to deal with your own health concerns. We are super excited to have you on board and would love to get you in the studio as soon as possible. The contract is with our contemporary Christian imprint, with an option to record a companion CD for the general market. Personally, I think it's a win-win. Your voice has crossover appeal that is through the roof. But like I said, whether you feel comfortable doing the general market release is totally up to you. This is going to be great. Once your stuff hits the airways, you are going to be big! I got a great feeling about this." Rob smiled and pushed the contract toward her.

Mackenzie reached for the papers, casting a glance at Mick that revealed a mixture of apprehension and excitement.

"It's okay, Mac," he reassured her. "Rob and I go way back. He'd never do anything to hurt you. I mean, he's a believer, after all. And he knows I'd break his arm if he did. Seriously,

I've read through the contract. It's fine; actually quite generous." Mick squeezed her hand.

"That's good enough for me," Mackenzie breathed. She picked up the pen and signed the paper in front of her.

Rob took the contract and stood. "Great! Let me me be the first to congratulate you on being Solar Music's newest recording artist!"

CHAPTER 30

The next morning, Mackenzie sat at the breakfast table with Morgan and her parents, sipping her coffee, munching her toast, and trying to delay broaching the topic that was weighing heavy on her mind. She dropped the half-eaten slice of toast onto her plate and blurted out, "I need your advice. Do you think I should resign from the Academy?"

After a moment of silence, her mother answered, "Dear, I'm sure you have prayed about this. What are your feelings? What are the pros and cons? Of course, we would hate to lose you but you must do what you feel the Lord would have you to do."

"You also have to do what is best for you and Morgan," her father put in.

Mackenzie picked up her coffee and sipped at it to give her time to formulate her words. "I need to be in Nashville in two weeks. Rob wants to see my songs; you know, the ones I've written. He also wants me to record a CD of love songs like I sang the other night. I need your input on that too. As far as resigning, I just don't know. I mean, I'm going to be really busy with the recording schedule, and I'll have to be out of town a lot. And it's not like I'll need the money from teaching—the advance was, well, significant to say the least."

Her father grinned. "It sounds to me like you already have your answer. If all you're waiting on is our blessing, you've got it. But we still have you for two weeks, until you leave for Nashville, right?"

Mackenzie blew out a relieved sigh, then pressed forward with her questions.

"Now about the secular music…"

"Does it involve performing in nightclubs," her father interrupted.

"Oh no," she countered. "No, I told Rob I would not do that. It may mean touring with some other mainstream artists, but not in night clubs."

Her mother patted her hand. "I think you need to be careful not to get sucked into something that vexes your spirit. The real questions are; what do you want to do, and what do you feel God would have you do?"

Mackenzie nodded and pushed the dishes away. "I think I would like to do both CDs; one for the Christian market and one for the general market. In both cases I'll be singing about love. What could possibly be wrong with that?"

"Then honey, do it," her mother smiled. "Just remember, we are proud of you and we love you."

Mackenzie joined Patty for dinner that evening at their favorite café. They made small talk while waiting for their meal to be served, but Patty couldn't contain her curiosity.

"So, Rob told me Mick is in New York on business. Are you missing him?"

"Of course I miss him," Mackenzie confessed. "But I just have these issues I need to resolve first. I envy you Patty. You've been hurt before, yet you don't seem to have any problems with trust. How do you do it?"

"Everyone handles things in their own way," Patty said. "I didn't go through what you did. You didn't go through what I did. But in the end, if we keep our focus on God, we come to the same destination. You'll be okay." She decided to change the subject. "So, I hear you've resigned from teaching."

"Wow, news travels fast."

"Small town," Patty giggled. "Everybody knows everybody else's business."

The waitress brought their meal and Mackenzie filled her in as they ate their meal. "Life is about to get real interesting," she confessed. "But enough about me. Give me all the juicy details about you and Rob."

Patty grinned, "Mick has good taste in friends. We get along just fine and Jaime likes him, but we're in no hurry. He sort of has an issue like yours; an ex-fiancé hurt him a lot. Did you know he was engaged a few years ago?" Mackenzie shook her head. "Yeah. It seems she broke it off when Rob decided to start Solar. She thought he was crazy to leave his high paying job in corporate America to start his own company. Oh well. Her loss; my gain. When you work this through Mac, and you will, you will see what a catch you have. Hey, what's not to like? He's a believer; he's gorgeous; he's ridiculously rich… and he's crazy about a certain redhead I know."

Mackenzie smiled. Mick truly was a one-of-a-kind. She just wished she could get past her own insecurities and commit. *No use whining about what isn't happening, when all this great stuff is going on,* she thought.

"I wish you could come with me to Nashville," she said aloud. "I could use a cheerleader in my corner."

"I'm pretty sure you'll have plenty of cheerleaders in Nashville," Patty laughed. "But I have a job, and a kid and a man who just opened an office in town. I do expect a couple tickets to your first concert, though."

Mackenzie smiled, "You've got it, Baby."

CHAPTER 31

The plane touched down at Nashville International Airport. Mackenzie felt like she should pinch herself. *Surely this is a dream and I'm bound to wake up soon.* Darla rearranged her schedule so she could be with Mackenzie for at least the first leg of her new adventure, and Patty had graciously offered to keep Morgan for the week. A limo was waiting to shuttle them to the Hermitage Hotel in downtown Nashville. Mackenzie felt like a peasant girl in a fairy tale who suddenly discovered she was a princess. She was dazzled, and even a bit overwhelmed. She was not used to being treated like royalty.

"I'm so glad I could come with you," Darla said as they settled into their hotel room. "This is like a vacation for me, and I'm so excited about getting to see you record. It's like a dream!"

Mackenzie nodded, lost in thought as she pondered how all of this had come to be. *God, you have blessed me so much. I just wish I could get past this fear inside me. One day, Lord. Please let it be soon.*

She was jostled from her reverie by the jangle of her cell phone. Mackenzie grabbed it, "Hello."

"Hi Mac, just wanted to let you know I'm thinking of you. Knock 'em out tomorrow." Mick's deep voice resonated in her ear and warmed her inside.

"Thank you, Mick," she said. "I'm glad you called. How are things in New York?"

"Ah, you know. New York is New York. I miss you and wish I were with you. But I'll be back in Winston next Wednesday."

The conversation was interrupted by a knock at the door. Darla motioned that she would answer it. When she returned, she was carrying an arrangement of two dozen long-stemmed red roses.

Darla held them out toward Mackenzie, with a knowing grin on her face. "From…who else?" she said as she read the card.

"Oh Mick," Mackenzie drew in a breath. "The roses are gorgeous. Thank you!"

"You're welcome. I gotta go. Duty calls. Have fun storming the castle," Mick said. "And if you need anything at all, just let me know, got it?"

Mackenzie smiled. "You've got it, Baby."

She disconnected the call just as the room phone rang. The concierge informed her that her limo was waiting. *My limo*, Mackenzie giggled to herself. *This really is too much.*

She and Darla climbed into the long, black limousine and she struggled to keep the butterflies in her stomach from churning into a hornets' nest. The car pulled up to the nondescript building on Nashville's historic Music Row, and Mackenzie swallowed hard. Some of the biggest names in country music had recorded in this faded, two-story brick building, and she was about to begin her career as a recording artist here. She was overwhelmed and more than a bit humbled.

Mackenzie gave her name to the receptionist and a moment later a tall man with a bushy beard wearing faded jeans approached her, his hand extended. "Mackenzie? I'm Jack Young, your engineer." He flashed her a broad smile. "We've already laid down the scratch tracks with the drums, bass and guitars. We'll get your vocals, then add the orchestration later. Ready to rock 'n' roll?"

Darla scrunched up her brows. "I thought this was going to be a CD of Christian songs, not rock and roll."

Jack laughed. "It's just an expression," he explained. "It just means, 'get started.' But full disclosure here, I think you'll find quite a bit of rock 'n' roll in Christian music these days."

"Oh," Darla said.

"Well, I'm definitely ready to roll," Mackenzie grinned. "Let's do it."

For the next four days Mackenzie poured her heart and soul into her vocals. It was an experience unlike anything she had ever encountered before. As good as she was, she discovered in the professional world of music recording, there was no such thing as a one-take-wonder. Every song was recorded, and re-recorded and recorded again. Small phrases were repeated multiple times to make sure every note was pristine, every word pronounced exactly right, every breath in its place. It was exhausting work, and by the end of the first session she was convinced she must be the worst singer ever if they had to do that many takes.

"This is phenomenal, Mackenzie," Jack said as she walked out of the recording booth. "You are amazing. Are you sure you've never recorded before?"

"Are you kidding," Mackenzie was almost in tears. "I thought I must be terrible with all the redos."

"Oh, no," Jack smiled. "You're knocking it out of the park. We've almost got the lead vocals for the first track laid; all in the first session. You have no idea how rare that is. We usually spend that much time on the first verse, even when we're working with seasoned pros. Now, how's about we grab some chow? San Antonio Taco Company is close and they make the best Mexican food in Nashville."

Mackenzie looked at her mother. "What do you say, mom. You up for some tacos?"

"I never say 'no' to tacos," Darla nodded.

Recording was a world apart from teaching, yet Mackenzie felt completely at ease; as if she belonged. The week flew by, and although she was exhausted at the end of each session, she also felt inexplicably exhilarated.

Friday's session ended early and Jack offered to treat for supper. Mackenzie suggested the Old Spaghetti Factory on 2nd Avenue, and they agreed to meet at 7 p.m., giving Mackenzie and Darla time to freshen up.

Nashville's trendy downtown was filled with tourists and locals out for a night on the town. They took the time to buy a few souvenirs while they waited for their table to be available. The meal was delicious, and the portions were twice as much as Mackenzie could eat. The conversation was light and engaging. By the time the waitress brought a steaming pot of spiced tea to the table, she felt more relaxed and contented than she could remember.

"This has been such a productive week," Jack said. "We have really been in a groove, and honestly, I hate to see it come to an end. When you've got momentum like this, it's always best to just keep it rolling. I don't suppose you could stay another week or two?"

Everything in Mackenzie leaped at the idea. She was in her element, as if she had finally discovered what she had been put on this earth to do.

"Mom, what do you think?"

"I think, as appealing as that sounds, you've got a daughter at home who is being kept by a friend," Darla admonished. "And I've got a husband who needs looking after."

Mackenzie shook her head, her red curls bounced around her face. *What am I thinking?*

"Of course. You're right mom," she said. "Jack, it's a wonderful offer, but as much as I'd love to continue on, right now I'm afraid we must get home. We'll pick up where we left off next time."

Jack nodded. "I get it. It was just a shot in the dark."

They finished their meal and Jack dropped Mackenzie and Darla at the hotel. "The limo will be here bright and early to take you to the airport. I'll let Rob know where we stand on the recording progress. Until next time!"

John Austen met them at the airport, holding Morgan in his arms. The toddler wriggled and bounced when she saw her mommy walking down the concourse. John put her on the floor and she ran full tilt into Mackenzie's arms. After many hugs and kisses, Mackenzie pulled a stuffed country bear from her bag and handed it to the squealing child.

"You two seem tired. I didn't know recording was so tiring." John pulled his wife into a fond embrace. "You can tell me all about it on the way home."

The next two weeks were a blur for Mackenzie. Without her regular teaching job, Mackenzie became involved in the local chapter of the American Diabetes Association. She even considered helping the organization start a summer camp for diabetic kids. Morgan had a few bouts of low blood sugar, but the pediatrician assured her it was not uncommon for young patients, and her own diabetes seems controlled, at least for the time being.

Mick was away on a business trip, but was due back tonight. She was surprised by how much she missed him. She could hardly wait for the evening. He was coming for dinner and she had a big surprise for him. *I sure hope he likes it,* she thought.

She spent the day putting the finishing touches on the meal, cleaning areas of the house that didn't need cleaning, and primping just a bit. *No reason I have to look dowdy, just because we're spending the evening at home,* she reasoned. She switched on the coffee maker and placed a tray of sugar-free cookies on the kitchen table as the doorbell chimed.

"I'll get it," Darla called from the living room.

Mackenzie took a moment to check her reflection. Not bad, she grinned. A moment later, Mick entered the kitchen carrying Morgan.

"Hello Mac, you look great this evening," he leaned in and placed a kiss on her cheek. "I feel like I haven't seen you in forever. How do you like being a rock star?"

Mackenzie's smile lit up the room. "I'm hardly a star – of the 'rock' or any other variety," she laughed. "But I do love the process. Rob seems to be pleased with the progress we're making. They are booking a few regional concert appearances in the next few months. Nothing big; just a couple of songs to open the show for some more well-knowns artists, just to get my name out there. I've even had a few interviews. Oh, and this is for you." She pulled a small package from the table and handed it to him. "For the man who has everything, here's something maybe you don't have."

Mick took the package. "You didn't have to buy me anything Mac."

"Actually, I… uh… didn't buy it," her cheeks flushed. "I… made it. In Nashville."

Mick ripped the paper from the package to reveal a jewel case with a silver CD inside.

"Rob encouraged me to write some of my own material."

Mick read the hand-written title information—*"You've Got It, Baby!" by Mackenzie Austen.* "Wait. You mean, you wrote…"

"Well, you don't have to look so surprised," she giggled.

"Where's the CD player? I've got to hear it."

"Don't get too excited," Mackenzie warned him. "It's just the rough cut. It still has to be mastered. But Rob says he thinks it could be the first radio single."

"Mac, this is fantastic," he said. He was afraid if his grin grew any larger it would split his face in two.

"And I think someone else has a present for you, too," Mackenzie winked. "Morgan, bring Mick his present, please." Morgan, who had been peeking around the corner, tore into the room as fast as her chubby little legs could carry her, carrying a brown paper shopping bag.

"For you, Mick!"

Mick reached into the bag and pulled out a picture frame holding a childish drawing that Mick could not decipher. He placed it on the table and pulled the little girl into a big embrace.

"Thank you, baby. It's beautiful!"

"Sweetie, why don't you tell Mick what everything in the picture is?" Mackenzie smiled.

The child pointed to a brown object in the corner of the drawing. "That my bear," she explained. She pointed to a blue scribble and said, "Mommy's mi'phone." Finally, she placed her index finger on a black and red blob. "Gringlay," she laughed.

Mick shot Mackenzie an inquiring look.

"She wanted to draw a picture of our favorite toys," Mackenzie explained. "Her favorite bear, my favorite toy, my microphone and," she smiled, "your favorite toy, 'you know who.'"

Mick hugged Morgan again. "I'm going to put this on my fireplace mantle. Thank you. Thank you this much!" He threw his arms open wide which prompted the little redhead to shriek with delight.

"There's one more thing in the bag," Mackenzie prompted.

Mick reached inside and pulled out what appeared to be a black ball of yarn.

"I hope it fits," she said. I had to guess at the size."

Confusion clouded Mick's expression as he examined the hollow ball. He turned it over. Red letters spelled out 'Gringolet.' Enlightenment started to settle in.

"Is this what I think it is?"

"Well, I needed something to do on the plane ride back from Nashville," Mackenzie laughed. "You might be the only man in town with a personalized gearshift knob cozy."

Mick threw back his head and laughed. "On behalf of my Corvette, I thank you. Now, I really want to hear this song!"

They went into the living room where John had a fire going to ward off the early November chill. Mackenzie slid the CD into the player, then sat down next to Mick as the strings began to swell. Mick closed his eyes and allowed the music to wash over him. He didn't open them again until the music stopped.

Mackenzie was staring at him intently, unconsciously biting her lower lip. "So, what do you think?"

"What do I think?" He turned to look into her eyes and thought his heart my burst. "I think…" He stood and applauded. "That's what I think."

"You really liked it? You aren't just saying that?"

He laughed out loud, "I think one of the smartest things I have ever done was to introduce you to Rob."

"And I think it's time to eat," John interrupted.

The evening passed with light conversation and much laughter. Darla offered to put Morgan to bed, and John retired to his study to prepare his next sermon. Mick and Mackenzie settled into the loveseat in the living room and stared into the fading embers of the fire.

"Mackenzie," Mick whispered as he stretched his arm around her shoulders. "You make me feel… I don't know… happy. But more than happy. You make me feel, alive."

She cocked her head sideways in that fetching manner that Mick loved. But this time she leaned into him. She leaned further until her lips met his and she brushed them with a tender kiss.

"I try to say it Mick," her voice trembled. "I do." A rogue tear trickled down her cheek. Mick caught it with his fingertips.

"Would it help," he whispered, "if I said it to you? Mackenzie, I love you."

Mackenzie shook her head, her red curls tickling his nose. "I want to say it. I just can't. Not yet," she sniffed. A sudden chill ran down her spine and she leaned back, afraid her moment had come and she had slammed the door on it. "Can you be patient with me?"

A deep sigh escaped from his chest. He drew her back to him in a sweet embrace. "There's no one else for me. Whenever you are ready, I'll be waiting." He gave a light chuckle and added. "I mean, after all, how many guys have a girlfriend who knits them a gearshift knob cozy for their sports car?"

CHAPTER 32

Mick watched the snowfall from his kitchen window. It was 9:00 a.m. on a Thursday in early December. Mick had been up since 5:00. He had already worked out, had his customary Bible study and prayers, showered and dressed for the day. Now was his time to enjoy a quiet cup of coffee and share a few moments with the Wall Street Journal. He was rudely interrupted by the cheery jangle of his cell phone.

"Hello?"

"Good morning, Mick. How's sunny Colorado this morning?"

"Gordon," Mick laughed, recognizing the voice on the other end of the line. "*Sunny* Colorado is about as sunny as I suspect New York is right about now. But the powder is deep and just right for skiing."

"Stop it. You're breaking my heart," Gordon retorted. "Remember a few months back when you asked me to look into Mackenzie's ex? Well, it's taken a bit, but I think I have the information you asked for. I know you thought he might have some connection to the Costino trucking family in New York, but that doesn't appear to be the case. I can keep digging if you want.

"Also, I've arranged for Lambert Foundation to establish a diabetes camp in Winston. The program will be administered jointly through the hospital and church. It's a stupid question, but I assume this camp has something to do with the famous Miss Austen?"

Mick exhaled deeply, "Yes sir."

"That girl is everywhere," Gordon chuckled. "TV, billboards, you can't turn on the radio without hearing that song of hers, *You've Got It, Baby!* Mick, I know how you feel about her. And I know how hard it has been for you to wait for her. All I can say is, I'm praying for you."

"Thanks Gordon, that means a lot. Yeah, it's a bit frustrating. It's one place where neither the Lambert name or checkbook can help."

"Well, as your Grandfather always used to say; 'Faith moves mountains when money can't.'

Mick nodded and ended the call. He took a swig of coffee and grimaced. It had grown cold during his conversation. He poured himself a fresh cup, then tried to read his newspaper, but to no avail. He couldn't stop thinking about the events of the previous night.

With a gathering of friends after church, Patty and Rob had announced their engagement. They had already set the date; January 12th, Patty's birthday. Of course Mick was happy for them, but he couldn't help feeling a twinge of envy.

Mackenzie was in LA and he missed her terribly. She had a couple of concerts scheduled and a TV appearance, then she was off to Dallas for three more engagements. *At least she got to take Morgan with her this time,* he mused. *Eight more days til she comes home. It shouldn't be this hard.* Mick was still wallowing in self-pity when his cell phone rang again.

"Hi Mick," a bright, shimmering voice beamed from the phone. He could envision her smile and the tilt of her head.

"Mac! Boy, do I miss you. I am having some serious Mackenzie withdrawal."

Mackenzie laughed. "Silly, I miss you too. But don't tell anyone, Okay?"

They chatted for awhile about the beautiful weather in LA, and how the concert tour was going, and how exciting it was that *You've Got It, Baby!* had crossed over onto the pop charts. The conversation stalled for a moment and there was an uneasy silence before Mackenzie shifted topics.

"Mick, I need to ask a favor. I was wondering... I know you've already done so much for me and Morgan, but... I don't want to take advantage of you, but..."

"Just ask the question, Mac," he sighed.

CHAPTER 33

Mick and Rob watched the snow fall from their booth at The Rocky Café. Ever since Rob opened his office in Winston, the two friends tried to meet for breakfast once a week. It got tricky since they both traveled extensively. This was one of those opportune moments.

"So Mick, why don't you just go with Mackenzie when she goes on the road?"

Mick sipped the hot coffee and shot a wry grimace at his friend. "You mean like a groupie? Yeah, not gonna happen. I mean, sure, I want to be with her; but I don't want to be just another face in the crowd." He motioned to the waitress for refills, "Honestly, I'm envious of you, Rob. I can't help it. I just am."

"Envious of me?" Rob snorted. "What on earth for? You're the golden boy with the magic touch. Talk about the world beating a path to your door. What's the big acquisition Lambert Industries is making this week?"

"Hey, business is good, and I'm not complaining about that," he confessed. "But I do envy what you have with Patty."

Rob started to respond, but Mick held up his hand. "I know, I know; *love is patient; seeks not its own way; hardly notices when others do it wrong,* blah, blah, yada, yada. I love her, Rob. I really do. But this waiting game is wearing on me."

Rob just nodded and sipped his coffee. He had seen more

than his share of couples break apart due to the stress of the entertainment industry. He wasn't sure he could add anything to the conversation that would help.

"I understand she asked you to get personally involved with the diabetes camp."

"She just asked me to make some phone calls."

"Mm hm. *Lambert* calls," Rob grinned. "The kind people can't say no to."

"I'm not sure the Lambert name packs that much of a punch around here. If you haven't noticed, and I'm pretty sure you have since you own her record label, Mackenzie Austen packs plenty of punch on her own."

Rob grinned. Of course he knew. Mackenzie was Number One on multiple Billboard charts in both the contemporary Christian and general markets. She was making lots of money for Solar Records.

"Yes, sir. The girl can sing," he said.

As if on cue, 'It's Magic,' the new radio single from Mackenzie Austen began to play over the café's radio.

"I rest my case," Rob laughed.

Mackenzie settled back in her seat. *I could get used to this*, she sighed to herself. Flying first class beat the pants off of coach. She snuggled Morgan close as the little girl drifted off to sleep. Outside the 727's window was darkness, the bright lights of LA fading in the distance. She closed her eyes and allowed her thoughts to drift.

The arena had been packed tonight. The Jam Tour featured some of the biggest names in Gospel and contemporary Christian music – what the media referred to as an all-star cast.

Mackenzie felt humbled just being on the same stage with them. The most amazing thing was discovering that although she had admired those people for years, even put them on a pedestal, they were human. They were people, just like her, with faults and fears and imperfections. Some were sweet and friendly; others were aloof and stand-offish. Some were pursuing their ministry as if their lives depended on it. Others were just doing their job. But they were all pressing forward. Just like her.

It will be good to see Wendy again, she thought. She drifted into sleep as the plane winged its way toward Dallas.

CHAPTER 34

The studio lights were warmer than Mackenzie expected. She tried to calm the butterflies that fluttered in her stomach while she settled onto the couch on the set of the *Good Morning, Dallas!* television show. Lynn Montgomery, the show's host, was a leggy brunette in her early forties. At once professional and personable, she made it a point to make her guests comfortable on camera.

"Just be yourself, Mackenzie," she encouraged. "You'll be great."

"Four, three, two, and…" the producer counted down.

"Good morning, Dallas!" Lynn smiled into the camera. "My guest this morning is a phenomenal new singer who burst onto the music scene, literally out of nowhere to take the country by storm. Six months ago, no one had even heard of her; and now, unless you're living under a rock, you not only know her name, chances are you're singing along to her songs on the radio. Of course I'm talking about chart topping recording artist, Mackenzie Austen!"

The studio audience burst into spontaneous applause. *At least they applauded and cheered in response to the signs being held up by production assistants,* Mackenzie thought, a wry smile creasing her face. *It's still amazing to see how the entertainment industry operates, now that the curtains have been pulled back.*

"Good Morning, Mackenzie. I was at your concert at

Longhorn Auditorium last night, and I've got to tell you, girl, you were fantastic!"

"Thank you," Mackenzie smiled.

"The song that started it all for you, is *You've Got It, Baby!* It's soared up to Number 1 on multiple charts, including Billboard's Hot 100 Pop Singles. That's quite a feat for a debut artist. You wrote that song, right? Tell us the story behind the song."

Mackenzie giggled and cocked her head. "You've Got It, Baby! was a catch phrase that my little girl, Morgan used to say whenever I would ask her to do something for me. It became something very special, and I wrote the song as a gift to a person who did something very special for me and Morgan. Honestly, it was supposed to just be a gift for that person. I never expected to record it, and I certainly never expected it to have the success it has achieved."

"Ooh, someone special," Lynn cooed. "Can you tell us who that special someone is?"

Mackenzie felt a warm blush rise onto her cheeks. She grinned and shook her head, her red curls bouncing playfully around her face. "This is probably not the right time to reveal that. But when the time is right, I promise, you'll be the first to know."

"You're all my witnesses," Lynn indicated the studio audience. "We get the exclusive when Mackenzie Austen make the big reveal, hopefully in the not too distant future."

The production assistants held up their signs and the audience cheered and applauded. Lynn shifted to a different line of questions.

"Mackenzie, while we were getting to know each other this morning before the show, you mentioned that you felt God created you to sing. What does that mean?"

"It's kind of like in that old movie, *Chariots of Fire*, when Eric Liddle said, 'God made me fast. And when I run, I feel His pleasure.' I don't really know how to describe it. It's not like I heard the audible voice of God or anything. But, I do believe it was God who gave me my voice. And when I sing, I feel His pleasure."

Lynn Montgomery smiled. "And when you sing, we feel His pleasure as well. So, would you sing for us now?"

Mackenzie nodded. She stood and crossed to the single microphone stand in the middle of the stage floor. There were no musicians. It was just her, singing *Amazing Grace* acapella.

When she finished, there was no need for the production assistants to lift their signs. The studio audience rose as one, and filled the room with thunderous applause.

"That was an unusual interview this morning," Wendy said as she placed a platter of homemade oatmeal cookies on the table. "So, mom tells me they want you to sing in a movie? How cool is that?"

Mackenzie chuckled and shook her head. "Kinda yes and no. It's a musical, but the actress they cast in the lead role can't carry a tune in a bucket. They want me to do the singing and the actress to lip-sync." She reached for one of the still-warm cookies. "Sugar-free, right?"

"Of course," her sister confirmed. "Speaking of this morning's interview, how are things between you and you're *special someone*? Any changes I should know about?"

Mackenzie took a long swig of coffee to wash down the cookie. "Not much to report, sis. Mick is great. He's patient and sweet and says all the right things at all the right times. I know he wants to take the relationship to the next level… but I can only do what I can do."

The conversation was interrupted by a whining Morgan who toddled into the room. Wendy reached for her but the toddler leaned away, dropped down onto the floor and wailed.

"What's wrong, baby? You don't want to cuddle with Aunt Wendy?"

Mackenzie gathered her into her arms. "Poor little thing, she's worn out from all the travel. So much excitement." She settled Morgan onto her lap and gently rocked. "It's just one more day, and we'll be heading home, baby."

Morgan snuffled softly, and within a few moments was asleep. Mackenzie carried the child to her bed, then came back to the table.

"It's been a busy week," she blew out a deep breath. "She's exhausted."

"Mackenzie," Wendy said. "Perhaps you should consider making some arrangements for Morgan. She's still a baby, and she has diabetes. Traveling has to be hard on her. And it can't be much easier on you."

Mackenzie bristled at the suggestion. From the beginning she was determined that being Morgan's mommy was more important than being a recording artist. But merging those two careers was proving more difficult than she had imagined. At last she nodded in reluctant agreement.

"I'll talk to Rob when we get back to Winston. I've got eight weeks before my next show. Maybe we can come up with a happy compromise."

CHAPTER 35

"Mommy, Mommy! Mick's here," Morgan tore into Mackenzie's bedroom, squealing with excitement. Mackenzie slipped on her heels and picked up her daughter. The truth was, she felt just as giddy on the inside as her young daughter appeared on the outside.

"Wow, you look gorgeous," Mick whistled when she walked into the living room. She twirled to show off the chic red pantsuit. Her hair was pulled back into a gentle twist, and her makeup was understated, demure and elegant – incorporating a few tips she had learned from the professional makeup artists while on the road.

"Well, you look pretty GQ yourself, Mr. Lambert."

She reached for her coat and Mick helped settle it around her shoulders, allowing his hands to linger on her arms for a moment longer than absolutely necessary.

"Drive careful," Darla admonished. "It's coming down hard out there."

"Will do, Mom," Mick said as he bent over and hugged Morgan goodnight. "I brought the Jeep for good measure."

"You be a good girl for grandma and grandpa, okay? I'll see you in the morning," Mackenzie added as she hugged her little girl.

Heavy snow was falling; great, big, fat snowflakes that would add to the ten inches already accumulated on the ground. Mick opened the door and helped Mackenzie up into the Jeep. He eased behind the wheel and started the engine. She turned toward him as the heater filled the cab with warmth.

"Since when did you start calling my mother, 'Mom?'" A bemused look crossed her eyes. "Do you know something I don't? 'Cause this would be really weird if it turns out you're the long lost brother I never knew I had."

Mick chuckled. "It's something I've done since I was a teenager. When I started dating a girl, I always asked the mother if I could call her 'Mom.' I figured, if I got in good with the mother, I didn't have to worry as much about the dad. Your mom seems to like it."

Mackenzie cocked her head and looked at him. It hadn't occurred to her that Mick may have had his own share of relationships with girls before he met her. She couldn't help the twinge of jealousy that gripped her heart.

"I can't begin to tell you how much I have missed you," Mick said as he negotiated the road. "I thought you would never get back here." He reached over and took her hand. "I saw that interview on *Good Morning, Dallas!* You were great, but I'm confused. Why didn't you tell them who you wrote *You've Got It, Baby!* for?"

Mackenzie's lips twisted into a grimace. "You know how rumors fly in the entertainment industry. I don't want your name bandied about in tawdry gossip rags. Besides, I told them in due time."

"I'm pretty sure *Good Morning, Dallas!* doesn't qualify as a tawdry gossip rag," Mick smirked. "And for the record, I have no problem whatsoever with having my name linked with yours."

Mick wheeled the Jeep under the portico and tossed the keys to the valet. Romano's was packed as usual on a Friday night, but Mick had a table reserved and the maitre d' ushered them in, bypassing the cadre of diners waiting to be seated. More than one person pointed at Mackenzie and whispered to a companion as they passed by.

"So, this is what it's like dining with a celebrity," he grinned as he held her chair.

"Cut that out," she retorted. "I'm the same girl I was when you first met me. Nothing has changed in that department."

Mackenzie grabbed her meter to enter a bolus of insulin before the meal.

"Some things have changed, Mac," he replied, indicating the pump. "How are you doing with that thing? Any problems on the road; I mean with your schedule and all?"

"The pump is working fine," she said. "It took a little getting used to, and I've put on a bit of weight."

"It looks good on you," Mick grinned. "I like a woman with some meat on her bones."

"Not the response most women want to hear, Mr. Lambert," Mackenzie shot back. "But for the record, Dr. Vogan agrees with you. She said I needed to gain a few pounds. Honestly, I'm more concerned with Morgan than with myself. All the traveling really wears on her. But when I'm on the road without her, I miss her like crazy. Sometimes I think I'm a terrible mother."

They were interrupted by the waiter bringing their salads. Mick reached for Mackenzie's hand and said, "I think you are a wonderful mother. Look, no job is perfect. Travel is a part of life for millions of people, fathers and mothers. At least you have the luxury of choosing when you're going to be away, and you have an excellent support group to help care for Morgan while you're on the road."

She nodded and forced a smile. "Thank you, Mick." She

sipped her coffee. "What are you doing for Christmas? You know you're welcome to spend it with us." She cocked her head and gave him that smile that always melted his heart. "You love redheads, right? Well, I know a couple of redheads who would love to share your company for the holiday."

Mick smiled back at her, his heart climbing into his throat. "Of course I will," he replied.

"Order me a piece of sugar-free strawberry pie, if it's not too much."

Mick chuckled. "You realize you are the least costly woman I have ever dated."

Mackenzie's expression was unreadable. *And you're the most costly man I've ever dated,* she thought.

"Dance with me?" she breathed.

"I'd love to," he whispered back.

The pianist was playing an old, romantic ballad from the 40's; 'A Nightingale Sang in Berkeley Square' Mackenzie thought. She led Mick onto the dance floor. He held her in his arms, swaying gently to the music. As they slow danced she sang softly. Mick thought that perhaps she was singing only to him. He was in paradise.

The music ended and applause erupted from the other diners. Mackenzie looked around the room, surprise etched across her face. She hadn't realized she was singing loud enough for anyone else to hear; her focus had been completely on Mick. She held her left hand up to acknowledge the crowd, bowed, and allowed Mick to lead her back to their table.

"Yeah, this is *definitely* what it's like dining with a celebrity," he laughed.

The strawberry pie arrived and the waiter freshened their coffee.

Mick shook his head and smiled at her.

She tilted her head, unable to decipher the look he gave her. "What?"

"I like dancing with you," he said.

His answer stirred emotions in Mackenzie that she was not expecting.

She blushed, and sipped her coffee to give her time to gather her thoughts.

"Mick, I have a serious question."

Mick raised an eyebrow and fixed his attention fully on her. "Fire away," he said.

"What do you really think of what I do? I mean, what do you think of what I do in relation to how our lives fit together, or might fit together, if it ever comes to that?"

Mick was stunned. It was not a question he had anticipated when he was getting ready for the evening.

"Well, I…uh…" he stammered.

"I love my life," Mackenzie interrupted his thoughts. "I love singing! I love singing at church. I love singing in arenas and auditoriums. And I love being in the recording studio. Yeah, it's tedious and repetitive, but it is amazing!" She took a breath and fixed her attention on the half-eaten sugar-free strawberry pie on her plate. She scooted a bite around with her fork. "Jared never wanted me to sing - not even at Dad's church. Jared didn't want me to have a career. He wanted me totally dependent on him. Jared didn't want me to have my baby." She looked up at Mick, her emerald eyes pleading. "I wouldn't be singing in arenas or signing autographs if it weren't for you, Mick. I know that, and I am so, so grateful. But now that I have it, I'm not sure I can give it up. Do you understand?"

Mick's brow creased and he shook his head in confusion.

"No," he answered. "I don't understand. I think I need to buy a vowel. I have no idea what you're trying to say."

Mackenzie took a deep breath. "Okay, let me start over. What I mean to say is, if I were ever to become Mackenzie Lambert…"

Mick's eyebrows climbed up to his hairline.

"I mean assuming you wanted me to become Mackenzie Lambert," Mackenzie added, "and…and you started to get jealous over my career and wanted me to give it up…I'm not sure I could do that. I think it would feel like when Jared wanted me to get rid of my baby."

Mackenzie's voice had dwindled to a low whisper and finally trailed off all together. She took a bite of pie and wiped a tear from her cheek with her free hand.

Mick sat silently for a moment, watching her, oblivious to the patrons in the still crowded restaurant. He waved away the waiter who was approaching with a fresh pot of coffee, then reached over and took her hand. Mackenzie lifted her eyes and looked into his.

"You are the best thing that has ever happened to me," he confessed. "When I first saw you in that parking lot, you were frantic. You needed me. But I'm pretty sure you don't need me now. Your career is on the cusp of superstar status. You're going to have more money than you know what to do with. And I love the way you have blossomed as a result of it all. The truth is, I like feeling needed. But I don't want to be needed for what I can give. I want to be needed for who I am." He drained his coffee cup, placed it back on the saucer, then reached across the table and took her hand. "The bottom line is this, Mackenzie. I don't want to change your life; I just want to be a part of it. I love you and I need you. And I hope that, at some point, when you're ready, you will need me too."

Mackenzie's heart screamed out, *I love you, too!* But a wounded place buried down deep in her soul refused to allow the words to form in her mouth. Instead, she merely nodded. She stood and pulled him to his feet.

"Dance with me?"

Mick didn't say anything. He just danced with her.

CHAPTER 36

Snow mixed with sleet came down hard, stinging Mick's face as he rushed through the hospital's emergency room entrance. Scanning the waiting room, he saw John Austen.

"Mick, over here." John Austen waved to him from across the room. I'm sorry to call you so early."

Mick nodded. This room was getting way too familiar.

"I was up. So, what happened?"

"We were in the kitchen having coffee, just like every morning, when Mackenzie commented that it was odd that Morgan wasn't awake yet. I mean, you know Morgan. That little firecracker is always up at the crack of dawn. Mackenzie went to check on her and couldn't wake her up. They've got her stable and are running tests. That's all I know. Mackenzie and Darla are with her. I've been out here, praying while I waited for you."

"Do you think its related to her diabetes?"

"I don't know," John's voice dropped. Mick could see the pain and worry in the older man's face. "I don't know what I would do if anything…"

Mick wrapped his arms around his friend's shoulders. "Don't even think it," he admonished. "We keep saying we trust God's plans for us are good. It's time to put feet to our faith. You've been waiting and praying. How about we pray together. You know, where two or more are gathered…"

The two men sat and prayed together, and while the situation hadn't changed, by the time Darla and Mackenzie walked into the waiting room there was a peace that filled the place that had nothing to do with the circumstances. Mackenzie saw Mick and rushed into his arms, embracing him as if her life depended on holding onto him. Mick said nothing; he just stroked her hair and let her breathe.

At last Mackenzie relaxed her hold on Mick. He offered her a handkerchief, which she accepted and used to dab at her eyes.

"Pneumonia," she blew out a self-reproaching breath. "The doctor said it was probably caused by a bronchial infection. The infection caused her blood sugar to spike." Her chin trembled. "She was complaining about being tired when we were in Dallas. I was so busy being a star that I didn't give it a second thought. What kind of mother am I?"

"Honey, stop it," Darla gently chided. "This is not your fault. You're a fantastic mother. Your child has diabetes. It's not a normal set of circumstances. We're all doing the best we can."

Mick kissed the top of her head and whispered, "Come on, sweetheart. Beating yourself up isn't going to help. And Morgan needs you to be strong."

Mackenzie sniffed, but nodded and made a weak attempt at a smile. Mick put a finger under her chin and lifted her face so he could look into her eyes. "Morgan is getting the best care in the state," he said. "She's going to be fine. This isn't a surprise to God."

"I know, Mick," Mackenzie replied. "She's just so little."

Mick smiled back at her. He felt…needed. "Can I see her. Does she need anything? What can I do?"

"Just pray for her and love her. They've got her designated for family-only visits for the time being, but I'm pretty sure the hospital will make an exception for you," Mackenzie barked a wry laugh. "She's sleeping right now so she won't know your there."

Winston General's Pediatric Intensive Care Unit was small, but well equipped. Morgan was hooked to a multitude of monitors, which made her look even smaller than she was. Mick felt helpless. The best he could do was lean over and place a kiss on the toddler's forehead. He wasn't sure his heart could ache any worse if Morgan was his own flesh and blood.

"Honey, we're going home for a bit," Darla said at last. "I know you want to stay with Morgan, but you need to eat and get some rest."

Mackenzie nodded. "I don't even have my purse with me." Mackenzie sat beside the hospital bed, resting her hand on her daughter's tiny body."

"I'll make a food run in a bit, and I'll drop by your house and pick up any necessaries. Just make me a list," Mick said.

"Honey," her father said, "soon as I get home, I'll get her on the prayer line and don't worry about tomorrow's service. I know you won't feel like singing."

"No," Mackenzie countered. "I'll be there." She fixed her father with a determined stare. "I once told someone, when I sing, I feel God's pleasure. But it's more than that. When I sing, I feel God's presence. And right now, I need to feel His presence. Me being here won't change Morgan; but me singing at church will change me. I need to be there, Dad. Please?"

"Alright, Honey," John said. A proud smile creased his face. He completely understood. It was in the pulpit that he most often encountered God.

Darla hugged Mackenzie. "I'll call Wendy and let her know

what's going on." She turned and gave Mick a kiss on the cheek on her way out of the room.

Mick pulled a chair up beside Mackenzie and sat down. Together they kept watch over the sleeping child.

"Mac, are you hungry?" Mick said at last. "It's almost noon."

"I don't have much of an appetite," Mackenzie sighed. "But I suppose I should eat something. It wouldn't do Morgan any good if I end up in the hospital beside her."

Mick nodded and walked to the hospital cafeteria. He returned a few moments later with a dish he thought might tempt Mackenzie's taste buds.

"Baked tilapia," he announced with a flourish. "One of your favorites, a diabetic delight, and more importantly, it was the daily special, so it didn't cost an arm and a leg."

Mackenzie grinned at his attempt at cheering her up. *He's trying so hard*, she thought. *I suppose I really should eat some of it, just to show my appreciation.*

Mackenzie took a bite of the delicate fish, then another. She was surprised to discover it was actually well prepared and quite tasty. *So much for the myth of bland, boring, yucky hospital food*, she thought. To her surprise, she found she was scraping the plate for the last bits of food. She looked up from her tray to find Mick still grinning at her. If anything the size of his smile had grown.

"Wow," he said. "I guess you were hungrier than you thought. Feel better now? Can I get you anything else? Refill your coffee?"

Mackenzie shook her head, and managed a small laugh. "No, I'm good," she answered. "I feel so much better. Actually, I would take a refill on the coffee."

"Another cup of Joe, coming right up," Mick smiled, and turned toward the nurses' station. He returned a moment later with two mugs filled with the steaming, aromatic liquid, and handed one to Mackenzie.

"M'lady," he said.

"Thank you, Sir Mick," she smiled back. She took a long sip and allowed the warmth of the coffee to radiate through her. "Good," she murmured. "Ya know, I'm beginning to think you just might be a handy man to have around."

Mick gave a mock bow, but inside something jolted. *All you have to do is say the word, and you can have me around for life,* he thought.

There was a sharp knock on the door, and a blond figure in a down-filled parka walked in.

"Mackenzie, we have got to stop meeting like this," Patty said as she embraced her friend. "Your mom called and filled me in. How's our little one?"

"Oh Patty, I'm so glad you're here," Mackenzie said. "Morgan is so sick. Dr. Brock says she'll be all right, but I can't help thinking what might have happened if I hadn't gone in to check on her when I did. I mean, what will happen if I'm away and she has another episode like this. I'm afraid."

Patty squeezed Mackenzie's hands. "I see a lot of sick kids in my line of work, but I've never seen a mother who loved her child, or took better care of her than you do. I can't say I know how you feel; I don't. Jaime's never been in the hospital. But if you need me girl, I'm here for you." Tears threatened to overflow from her eyes.

"Patty, please don't cry. You'll get me started again," Mackenzie snorted a laugh and hugged her friend.

"I've got to get to work, but I'll drop by and check on you after my shift," Patty said. "Your mom said you're still planning on singing in church tomorrow?"

"Yes, I will be there."

"Girl, I don't know how you do it. I'd be a puddle of mud by now," Patty said as she started to leave. She stopped at the door and turned back. "One piece of advice; get yourself some rest. This is gonna be a marathon, not a sprint."

Mackenzie nodded and Patty left just as the duty nurse entered the room to check on Morgan. She checked her vitals and entered the data on the electronic device. She looked at Mackenzie, then back down at the patient information on her device, then back at Mackenzie, her eyes wide.

"Your Mackenzie Austen!" she blurted out, then blushed. "I'm sorry. I've never really been this close to an honest-to-god celebrity before." She looked from Mackenzie to Morgan and commented, "She looks just like you; so petite, so pretty."

"I don't know about the celebrity part," Mackenzie said. "But I do try to be honest-to-God."

"I'm Janet, and I'll be here until this evening if you need anything," the nurse said. "Blood glucose level is coming down slowly. She's a little fighter. Dr. Brock's as good as they come. She's in good hands. Seriously, if you need anything at all, just press the button."

The nurse left them standing beside Morgan's bed. The snow pelted the window as the monitor beeped out its staccato rhythm. At last Mick announced his intention to drive to the Austen home and pick up Mackenzie's essentials.

"I suspect there is no chance of talking you into going home for the night?"

Mackenzie shook her head. "I couldn't Mick," she said. "I'd be worried sick every moment. It's going to be hard enough leaving her to go to service tomorrow."

Mick nodded. He took her hand and squeezed it hard, then

headed for the door. He was half way to the elevator when he heard Mackenzie's sweet voice wafting through the hall. A lump rose into his throat. The song was "I've Got a Crush on You," and he had heard Mackenzie sing it to Morgan many times before. He asked her about it once.

"It's her favorite song," Mackenzie explained. "I sang it to her the day she was born."

CHAPTER 37

Mackenzie is holding up well, Mick thought as he watched her sing with the worship band on Sunday morning. The worry that was evident in her eyes did nothing to diminish the power of her voice. If anything, she sang with greater passion and urgency than he had ever heard.

As soon as service ended, Mick ushered Mackenzie through the throng of well-wishers to his Jeep, and drove her back to the hospital. There was little change with Morgan, although her blood sugar level was continuing to decline. Dr. Brock advocated patience, which made Mick want to chew nails. Patience was not his strong suite.

He excused himself and wandered down the hall in search of the nearest coffee maker. He found one at the nurses' station and poured a cup for himself, and another for Mackenzie.

Once back to the room he passed the tall Styrofoam cup to Mackenzie. She took it with a rueful smile, and they stood silently, staring down at the unconscious child. Mackenzie reached down and touched her cheek. Mick watched, feeling more helpless than he ever had. The room was quiet; too quiet. The day wore on until dusk settled over the mountains. Outside the window the parking lot lights were starting to wink on. Everything appeared peaceful, serene…and cold.

Mackenzie brushed a tear from her eye as she silently prayed. Someone at the nurses' station had turned on the radio, and the sounds wafted across the hall and into the room; Mackenzie's voice crooning, '*You've got it, baby…*' Mackenzie looked into Mick's face and gave a weak smile. She turned her attention back to her little girl. "Come on, Baby. Wake up. Wake up for me."

Mick put an arm around her shoulders, and she pressed into him. He hated the circumstances that produced this moment, yet the feel of her body against his, pulling strength from him, made him feel more right than he ever felt. Mackenzie, collapsed into his arms and wept.

She was still weeping when a thin voice whispered, "Mommy? I'm thirsty."

Mackenzie stifled a scream. "Morgan? You're awake!"

CHAPTER 38

Mackenzie stopped at the nurses' station on the pediatrics floor. Morgan had improved enough over the past 48 hours that Dr. Brock released her from the PICU. There was a young nurse on duty that Mackenzie didn't recognize.

"Hi. I'm Mackenzie Austen. How is Morgan this morning."

The nurse looked up and did a double-take. Her eyes flew open wide and she blurted out, "Oh my god, you're her. When I saw Morgan Austen's name on our list it never occurred to me that she was related to Mackenzie Austen!"

A crimson flush rose up the young nurse's neck and stained her cheeks as the shock wore off and she suddenly realized she was on duty.

"I am so sorry," she apologized profusely. "I didn't mean to come across so unprofessional. I just never…I mean, I didn't expect…I mean, hoo boy…"

Mackenzie chucked and raised her hand to stop the flow of words. "It's okay," she soothed the flustered young woman. "I get that a lot."

The nurse took a deep breath and said, "She's doing much better. Dr. Brock made his rounds earlier this morning, and he was smiling when he left. I suspect he'll fill you in on all the details when he comes back through, but for now it looks like she's fighting her way back from the infection in her lungs. She's a sweet little thing, I can tell you that."

Mackenzie nodded her agreement, and headed for her daughter's room where she was greeted by a much improved Morgan, and rumpled looking Mick.

"Mommy, Mommy," the toddler squealed as she threw her arms out wide for a hug. Flowers, balloons, stuffed animals and coloring books filled the room.

Mackenzie picked her up. "Who loves you, Baby?"

Morgan giggled and pointed at her, "You do!"

Mick stretched wide, yawned and scratched, then pouted. "Hey, I'm the one who was here all night. Can I get some of that?"

Morgan giggled. "And you do, too," she crowed.

"You got that right," Mick laughed. "I sure do love you."

He gave Mackenzie a sweet peck on the cheek then excused himself. "I'm gonna go home and grab a shower and a shave, and maybe 40 winks," he said. "I need to check in with the office, and I'll be back later this afternoon."

Patty stuck her head in the room to say 'hi' before she started her shift. There was a glow about her that Mackenzie could not help but notice. *Being engaged to Robert Mann must agree with her,* she thought. Patty chattered about how much Jaime missed Morgan, and how the wedding plans were progressing, and how she and Rob were looking at a house right down the road from Mick's.

"Solar Records is doing great," she added. "I'm pretty sure you're the one who put them on the map. But I'm not gonna stop working. I like my job, and Rob's always having to fly to different parts of the country. Anyhow, I gotta get to work, girl. I'll stick my head back in after my shift, just to make sure they're taking good care of you. Bye!"

Mackenzie had to shake her head and chuckle. She wasn't sure her friend had taken a breath.

Lunchtime came and went, and Morgan was settling down for an afternoon nap when Mick walked in, followed by John and Darla.

"Grandma, Grandpa! Hug, Hug, Hug," Morgan bounced up and down in her bed, reaching her arms high above her head. The older couple were more than willing to accommodate her.

The conversation drifted from the growing church attendance - which John attributed at least in part to Mackenzie's growing notoriety; to the new teacher who had taken Mackenzie's place; to the political climate in Denver; and ended up with discussions about the Christmas season.

"Speaking of Christmas, what would you like Santa to bring you," Mick asked the little redhead. Morgan didn't even blink an eye.

"A mi'phone," she answered.

"A mi'phone?" Mackenzie raised an eyebrow. "You want... a microphone?"

"Uh-huh," was all she said. She picked up a hair brush from the nightstand, held it to her lips and began to sing, 'I've Got a Crush on You!'

When she finished, Mick applauded as the other adults shared confused stares.

"I want to sing like you," she pointed at Mackenzie.

"Must be in the gene," John laughed.

The young nurse interrupted the concert to give Morgan some antibiotics. She noticed the hair brush and asked, "Have you been combing your hair and making yourself all beautiful, like your mommy?"

"No," Morgan shook her head. "Singing."

"Oh," the nurse said as she took a glucose reading. "Would you sing for me?"

Morgan nodded and looked at her mother. Mackenzie picked the child up and placed her on her lap, then announced into the hair brush microphone; "Ladies and Gentlemen, this afternoon, live from Winston General Hospital Pediatrics floor, heeeere's Morgan!"

The other adults in the room applauded and Mick whistled as Mackenzie began to softly sing into Morgan's ear. Morgan held out the 'microphone' and joined in on the chorus. They finished the song amid raucous applause. The nurse grinned and shook Morgan's hand.

"That was wonderful," she gushed. "It's not too often a girl gets her own private concert in the hospital. Wait'll I tell the other nurses. They'll be green."

CHAPTER 39

Mick reached to shut off the alarm beside his bed before realizing the annoying buzz was coming from his cell phone. He fumbled for it, noticing it was 12:35 a.m. His eyes flew wide. Nobody called at this time of night unless something bad had happened.

Caller ID showed it was Mackenzie. His heart climbed into his throat.

He hit the answer button. "Hello? Mackenzie? Are you alright? Is Morgan alright? What's wrong?" he demanded.

"Oh, Mick, I'm so sorry. I didn't realize what time it was," Mackenzie answered. "I'm sorry to bother you. It's nothing. Everyone's okay. Morgan's okay. I'm sorry. It's not important. I'll call you in the morning."

"No way," Mick responded, a bit more harshly than he intended. "I'm awake now. It's fine. Let's talk. What's up?"

"I just…" she fumbled over her words as if unsure of how to say what was on her mind. "I couldn't sleep, and all these thoughts were rolling around in my mind, and it occurred to me that," she exhaled deeply "that if you and I were to… I know you haven't asked me or anything, but if you did, ask me to marry you…"

Mick held his breath.

"You need to know that I can't have any more children. During Morgan's birth there were…complications."

179

There was an uncomfortable silence that accented the darkness. Mackenzie bit her lip and waited.

Mick answered. "We've never really talked about it. And?"

Now it was her turn to leave the conversation hanging for a heart wrenching moment.

"I mean, doesn't that bother you, Mick?" she breathed. "You're a guy and guys want a son they can take to ball games, and to carry on the family name and…" her voice trailed off. "And I wouldn't want to be a disappointment to you."

Mick let out a relieved sigh. "Is that all?" He laughed, and immediately realized that was not the best response in the current situation. "Mackenzie, I love you. Period. And I love Morgan. I'm pretty sure that little girl will keep me more than busy enough. So, when the right time comes, and you're ready, there is nothing that will stand between us. Okay?"

There was another momentary silence, then Mackenzie whispered, "Okay."

"So, have I allayed your concerns? Is this a good time for me to ask you to marry me?" He heard her lilting laughter.

"What? You're gonna ask a girl the most important question of her life over the phone? I don't think so."

Now it was his turn to laugh, "I can't help but think that you only want me for my car. What is it Batman says, 'Chicks dig the car?'"

"Gringolet is pretty cool," Mackenzie giggled. "Good night, Mick."

It was nearly 1:00 a.m. Mick wasn't sure he'd be able to get back to sleep. But eventually he drifted off, and dreamed of a beautiful pair of green eyes.

∾

He pulled into the Austens' driveway the following morning in a new, four-wheel drive, extended-cab pickup "Hey! What is this?" Mackenzie asked as he opened the passenger door and helped her in. A sheepish grin crossed Mick's face.

"I've had my eye on it for a while now. I dropped by the dealership on the way over," he confessed. "So, do you like it?" He climbed behind the wheel, and backed it onto the street. "You said dark green was your favorite color. It's an automatic, and the four-wheel drive is just a push of this button. The Jeep's a standard, and you can't drive a stick, so I figured, this might... I mean... Well, do you like it?"

She stared at him, realization dawning. "You bought this... for me?"

"Well, yeah." Mick fidgeted. "It's got a great space in the back for a car seat so Morgan will be comfortable, and... I overstepped, didn't I?"

"Just a little bit," Mackenzie chided. "But she is a beauty. And you fight dirty, Mick Lambert!"

The snow was cold and the snow plows were fighting to keep the roads clear. Traffic was a a crawl, making the drive to the hospital a slow, but not unpleasant one. It gave them time to just be together, and talk.

"When I was in my teens, I thought it would be difficult to find a woman who would be interested in a guy like me," Mick said as he pulled into the on-ramp for the Interstate. He glanced at Mackenzie and saw her raise an eyebrow. "You know what I mean. I realize my money makes me a target for a lot of gold-diggers, but I'm talking about a girl who would like me for who I am, not what I have. Don't tell me you haven't thought about that."

"Yes, I have thought about it. Why do you think I called you last night?" She focused her green eyes on Mick as he passed a slow-moving sedan with Florida tags. *Some folks just don't know how to drive in snow,* she thought. "I've felt the same way; that no man would want me if he knew I couldn't give him children. It made me feel like a piece of me was missing. You don't feel that way about me, do you?"

Mick focused his attention on the road, grimly aware of the number of vehicles that had already slid into snow drifts on either side of the highway. *These are not good conditions to allow yourself to become distracted while driving,* he reminded himself.

"No," he answered. "Not at all. I haven't noticed anything about you that's missing." Then he added, "In fact, I'm pretty impressed with all your parts." He reached over and squeezed her knee.

Mackenzie swatted his hand away, but giggled nonetheless. She cocked her head and gave him an impish grin. "Keep your hands to yourself, Mr. Lambert, if you please," she chided, then her voice took on a more serious tone. "Actually, I thought you might run away when you found out. But you didn't." She flashed him a big smile. "That's another mark in the plus column for you. I think I might like almost as much as I like Gringolet."

Now it was Mick's turn to grin. "What can I say? Chicks dig the car."

Mick pulled into the Visitor's Parking lot at the hospital and they walked into the building side by side.

Darla Austen had spent the night at the hospital in Morgan's room to give Mackenzie the night off. The child was continuing to make progress. "Barring any unforeseen complications, I don't see any reason she can't go home soon," Dr. Brock informed them. "Maybe tomorrow, but more likely the day after tomorrow. Let's just keep an eye on her and see how things work out."

John Austen arrived shortly before lunch. Mackenzie and Mick slipped down to the cafeteria to grab a bite before Darla and John left. While they munched on salads, Mackenzie leaned toward Mick, and said sweetly, "Mick, you would do just about anything for me, wouldn't you?"

Mick gave her a deer-in-the-headlights look, and continued chewing his salad. He thought about saying, Of course, but with her voice dripping honey, he reconsidered and responded with a more tempered, "Well, yeah. Anything within reason."

"When we get back to Morgan's room let me check your blood sugar, I have my meter in my purse." Before he could say anything, let alone object, Mac placed a finger to his lips.

"Please understand, Mick, I know this sounds like I'm being unreasonable, and I don't want to be, but I've been blindsided by diabetes twice already this year; first Morgan and then myself. I'm not being paranoid. Really, I'm not. At least I don't think I am. Okay, maybe I'm being a little paranoid, but…"

Mick chuckled. "I don't think you're paranoid," he said, "I can understand how you must feel. Honestly, I am flattered that you are so concerned, but I'm fine."

Mackenzie leaned toward him, her green eyes locked on his. "You did say you would do anything for me, didn't you?"

"And you said *I* fight dirty," he groaned.

Chapter 40

Mick went home that afternoon emotionally exhausted. *Sitting around a hospital room all day is hard work*, he thought. He settled back in his favorite easy chair and picked up the newspaper, only to set it down again. He had little interest in what was going on in the outside world right now. His whole world was tied up in the well-being of two redheads.

The fire crackled blissfully in the fireplace and Mick gazed through the plate glass windows at the blazing sunset that was rapidly giving way to a darkening sky. A star winked on; then another. He closed his eyes and thought of Mackenzie's smile, the coquettish tilt of her head, the flash of her emerald eyes and the warmth of her laugh; and he fell asleep.

When he opened his eyes, he was in a hospital room. A long line of lab techs came into his room and drew blood, one after another, vial after vial. He just wanted to sleep every time he started to drift off, another nurse would wake him to test his blood sugar or to inject him with insulin.

He was famished, but when the orderly brought his lunch tray, it was nothing but bread and water. He called the duty nurse to complain about the meal. "I'm so sorry about the mix-up, Mr. Lambert," the nurse apologized. "We *did* make a mistake. We gave you too much bread." She snatched the bread and walked out of the room.

Mick startled awake, his heart racing. *Calm down, Mick,*

calm down! It was just a dream. He checked his arms for needle marks, just the same.

He picked up the poker and gave the embers a rough poke, causing a myriad of sparks to dance upward through the flue. *No way I'm going back to sleep; not after that dream,* he muttered to himself. *What I need is a strong cup of coffee.* He padded to the kitchen, turned on the coffee pot and checked his watch. *Only nine o'clock?* He whistled. *Feels like I've slept forever.* While he waited for the coffee to perk, he snatched his phone and hit the speed dial. He needed to hear a specific voice, and he needed to hear it now. Two rings were followed by a tired sounding, "Hello."

"Hey Mac," he fumbled over his words. He wasn't sure why he called; he just knew he had to. "I, uh… I just wanted to see how Morgan is. She was asleep when I left. And I want to see how you are."

"Morgan's doing great. The antibiotics are making her sleepy, but this is the last day for that. Everyone's gone home, and Morgan is asleep, so it's really quiet around here for a change." Her voice grew low and warm. "Me? I'm okay. I've been praying a lot; using the down time to try to write a few lyrics. Thinking about you."

Mick's mouth suddenly went dry and he had to swallow hard to get moisture back into it before he spoke again.

"Yeah, I've been thinking about you too," he said.

"The nurse is coming in to check on Morgan," Mackenzie said. "I should probably go."

"Okay," Mick said. "I'll come by tomorrow. Call me if you need anything."

"I will. 'Bye."

Mick ended the conversation and dropped the cell on counter.

Hearing Mackenzie's voice, even for a few moments, made him feel good inside, warm. He liked it.

He poured a cup of coffee, stirred in some sugar, and carried it back to his chair by the windows. He prayed as he stared into the darkness, with a million stars as his witnesses. *Lord, if this thing I have with Mackenzie is real, and if it's from You, I really need for it to move forward. If it's not from You, then You need to squash it and let me move on. This waiting game is about to kill me.*

Mick sipped his coffee while the stars winked at him, but there was no voice from on high telling him what to do. *Okay,* he thought, remembering one of his grandfather's favorite old saying. *When you don't get any new instructions, you just keep moving in the same direction until you do.*

He sat up and turned on the lamp. He picked up a note pad and made a short list of things he could do to help his two favorite redheads.

He had already been instrumental in helping found the diabetic children's camp coming next summer. But there was so much more he could do. This was his element—business and promotion. He scribbled furiously as more and more ideas popped into his brain. At last he stopped and perused his notes. He smiled. *I think Mackenzie is really going to be excited about this.*

Satisfied with his efforts, Mick turned off the light, returned his coffee cup to the sink, and headed for his bed. This time he slept without any disturbing night nurse trying to poke him with a needle.

The next morning Mick showered quickly and rushed to the hospital. He couldn't wait to show Mackenzie his plans.

Morgan was still asleep when he arrived at 8:00 a.m. Darla was already there.

Mackenzie met him at the door and gave him a warm hug. "You look lovely this morning Mac, as usual."

"I look like a mess," she replied, "But thanks anyway."

"Well, you look lovely to me," he said. "Hey, can we go down to the cafeteria and grab some coffee? I've some stuff I want to show you. Darla, do you mind?"

Darla waved the question away. "No worries," she smiled. "You two go and talk. I can hold down the fort."

Mick got the coffee while Mackenzie found an empty table in the far corner.

"So, Mr. Lambert," she said after taking a sip of coffee. "What's so important you had to drag me down here to talk about it?"

Mick grinned like a kid at Christmas time. "I have ideas… for the children's camp next summer." He pulled the folded sheet of notes from his pocket and handed it to her.

Mackenzie unfolded the paper and read, her eyes growing wider with each line. At last she handed the paper back to Mick. "You want to launch a three-day festival to increase diabetes awareness?"

Mick's head bobbed up and down like one of those little dogs Mackenzie had seen in the back of low-rider cars.

"The Lambert Foundation is a major sponsor for the camp, but I know there are other things we can do to bring diabetes to the people's attention, and maybe even make some money for the cause. A three-day fair would be a great way to build some excitement, and give back to the community, and raise awareness all at the same time. We could bring in some big-name entertainers, like, oh, I dunno, maybe Mackenzie Austen? I hear she's got a hit song on the radio. And I'm pretty sure Rob can get Solar Records behind it. So, what do you think?"

"What do I think?" Mackenzie leapt to her feet and planted

a big kiss on his mouth. "I think it's an amazing idea. I love it! I think you're a genius, and I think you are such a generous, kind-hearted man. And I think…I think I…"

Mackenzie collapsed back into her chair, threw her hands over her face and wept.

Mick's jaw dropped. He was flabbergasted. *What did I do wrong?* he wondered. Confused he reached toward her, then pulled his hand back, unsure of whether she would want him to touch her. "Mackenzie? I'm sorry. I don't know what… I mean, did I do something to upset you? I mean, I thought you'd like…"

"Oh Mick, I want to say it so damn bad!" she cried out. "I'm trying. I'm trying so hard."

Mick's confusion increased to a whole new level. "What?" he ventured. "What is it you want to say, Mackenzie?"

"That I love you," she whispered. She looked up at him with pleading eyes. "I really want to. I do. I just…can't get the words out. Not yet. Please don't leave. Please be patient with me?"

Mick breathed a sigh of relief. Fear that he had somehow overstepped his bounds faded. He knelt in front of her and took her hand. "I am not going anywhere," he promised. He placed his fingers beneath Mackenzie's chin and lifted her face until her eyes met his. "Hey, I'm not going anywhere. I promise. Okay?"

She sniffed, smiled and nodded. "You won't tell Dad what I swore, will you?"

Mick and Mackenzie walked hand in hand back to Morgan's room where they were met with unexpected good news - Morgan was being discharged. Dr. Brock wrote out a prescription for a children's strength pain killer, just in case Morgan experienced any residual discomfort, and signed the discharge papers.

"I'll get the truck and meet you outside," Mick said.

"No good," Mackenzie replied. "Morgan needs a car seat. We'll ride home with Mom."

"Oh, I guess I forgot to tell you," Mick grinned. "I had one installed in the back seat yesterday on my way home."

Mackenzie stood with her hands on her hips for a moment, then licked her finger and made an imaginary mark in the air.

Mick looked puzzled. "What was that?"

"Just putting another mark in the Plus column," she replied. "Mr. Lambert, you fight dirty."

CHAPTER 41

Mick lay awake in bed, and watched the snow falling outside his window. His thoughts drifted with the delicate flakes, swept to and fro by the whims of the wind. They settled at last on a certain petite redhead named Mackenzie Austen, a girl who was rapidly becoming America's next Sweetheart.

She had earned enough money from her personal appearances over the past few months to buy a new car, and she had picked out a new Corvette. Mick had helped negotiate the deal after finding an emerald green model with an eight-speed, paddle shift automatic transmission at a dealership in Boulder.

"I think you're going to like it," he said, admiring the Stingray's custom leather wrapped interior. "She looks a lot more comfortable than Gringolet."

"And she's a whole lot quieter," Mackenzie laughed. "Mom should be happy about that. Now, how 'bout lunch? My treat."

"Who am I to argue about a free lunch?" Mick quipped. They met at The Beef Rack restaurant and parked their 'Vettes side by side.

Mackenzie bounced on her toes all the way into the steakhouse. "I am so excited, Mick," she giggled. "Just think I will have my own Gringolet!"

"I dunno," Mick shook his head. "She looks more like a Guinevere to me."

"Guinevere," Mackenzie repeated. "I like it!"

I wonder how long before she works up the nerve to say she loves me? he thought as the snow continued its slow descent. I mean, she does love me…doesn't she? Of course she love me. She just can't say it. Patience, Lambert. Patience!

The old cartoon of two buzzards talking to each other in the desert crossed his mind. The caption read, "To heck with patience. I'm gonna kill something." Mick chuckled at the thought.

Mackenzie's popularity was continuing to skyrocket, but not in the fashion they had all envisioned. She was all over the pop charts, but her radio airplay on Christian radio had leveled off, and no one had a good explanation for why.

Rob didn't seem fazed by it. The Christian market was teensy compared to the general market, he explained. When it came to the music business, it was far better to be a medium-sized fish in a big ocean than a big fish in a small pond.

"Two monster radio hits have got the market clamoring for the CD release," he said. "We'll do a double whammy, releasing CDs to both the contemporary Christian and general markets at the same time. We've got the release date set for March 1. We're putting together a radio tour of the hottest stations in both formats; then we'll hit the festival circuit this summer; and I don't want to jinx it, but there's a lot of interest in adding you to the ticket for a multi-artist European tour this fall."

Mackenzie was overwhelmed by it all. Mick couldn't blame her. It was a lot to take in. In the space of six months she had gone from an unknown single mom, teaching elementary kids at a church school, to a bonafide internationally-acclaimed recording artist. It was enough to befuddle the wits of even a seasoned professional. That kind of success didn't come along everyday, and most people couldn't handle it.

Can you handle her success? The thought rose unbidden, and took Mick by surprise. He had been raised with money, success and power. In fact, he had never known life any other way. But Mackenzie was new to it all. He wasn't sure what it might do to her. And he wasn't sure he knew how to help her negotiate the potholes in this particular yellow brick road.

CHAPTER 42

Mick pulled his truck into the Austen driveway. Mackenzie was stomping down the walk before he even shut off the engine. He hopped out and opened the passenger door for her. She climbed into the truck without a word, but her eyes were flashing, and there was no smile on her face. He slipped behind the wheel, trying to figure out what he had done that ticked her off. "Are you all right?" he ventured.

"Just drive," she seethed.

Mick didn't know much about women, but he knew not to get between a mother bear and her cub, and he knew not to ask questions when Mackenzie had that look on her face. He drove in silence and waited for her to speak first.

"I had a little conversation with my parents this morning," she said at last. Mick could tell she was straining to keep her emotions in check. "It seems there are some malcontents in the church who don't appreciate my choice of material on the mainstream CD. They don't think it's 'God-honoring,' or 'it's not spiritual enough,' and they're questioning whether I've left my 'first love.' Oh, and God help us, someone saw us dancing to the 'devil's music' at Romano's. And it appears I'm getting way too full of myself because I dared to by a fancy sports car...with my own money that I earned, thank you very much. It's not like the piddly little stipend I get from the church for singing on Sunday mornings is going to pay for my hedonist lifestyle!" Her voice rose in both pitch and volume as she talked.

Mick wasn't sure if it was cathartic for her to keep talking, or if it was just adding fuel to the fire. He didn't know if she wanted his opinion, or if the better part of valor would be to just stay quiet and listen. Mackenzie seemed to have talked herself out, and silence reigned in the cab of the truck for a few awkward moments. He decided to risk asking a question.

"So, what are you going to do, and how can I help?"

Tears started leaking down Mackenzie's face; whether from anger, frustration or sadness, Mick wasn't sure. "I told Dad that if I was being such a big distraction to the congregation, maybe it would be best if I resigned my position at Faith Center and move away from here."

Mick was stunned. It was not the answer he had envisioned. "You mean, move out of your parents' house? Move your membership to another church?"

"I mean move to someplace where I don't feel like I'm living in a fishbowl," she turned her face away and stared out the window at the snow falling in lazy random patterns. "I've never lived anywhere else but Colorado. But I've started to see the world and now I realize there is so much more out there. Maybe LA, or New York, or even Nashville. That's where music is king. I don't know," she sniffed. "Maybe I just need a change of scenery."

He kept his thoughts to himself. *She'll ask when she wants my opinion,* he reasoned. He pulled the truck under the portico at Romano's, tossed the keys to the valet, and trotted around to help Mackenzie down.

"You look absolutely lovely this evening," he said as he escorted her into their favorite restaurant. Mackenzie's simple navy sheath dress and matching strappy heels perfectly accented the lovely red curls that framed her heart-shaped face.

The proprietor, Mr. Romano himself, greeted them, waving away the hostess. "Good evening, my friends, how are you?"

He led them through the dining room to the table Mick had reserved the day before. The fireplace was lit, casting a warm, inviting glow over the diners. On the raised platform a jazz trio was entertaining.

"Oh, Mr. Romano, they sound wonderful," Mackenzie beamed, "absolutely wonderful."

"It is all because of you, Missy Mackenzie," Romano responded. "Since you became famous, people demand live music, and one thing leads to another. Live music brings in more guests. More guests spend more money. Everybody is happy!"

A waitress appeared at their table and took their order, then moved on to attend to her other guests. Mick reached across the table and took Mackenzie's hand.

"You know if you really need a change of scenery, I have a suggestion."

Mackenzie pulled her hand back warily. "Mick; I can't go to a Justice of the Peace. Think how much that would hurt Daddy's feelings and…"

Mick laughed and cut her off, "I like the way you're thinking, but that wasn't a proposal. You had mentioned New York, and the Lambert Group keeps an apartment available in Manhattan for visiting muckity-mucks. It's a great place to lay low for a while; I mean, if you just need some time to get away and think. I know it's not a permanent solution, but…"

"Don't tempt me," Mackenzie reached back and grabbed his hand. "And thank you," she added seriously.

"For what?"

"For not chiding me, or telling me I'm behaving like a petulant child, or trying to give a boatload of free advice."

Mick nodded and smiled to himself. *Looks like you've done something right for a change, Lambert,* he thought. *Try not to screw it up, okay?*

The waitress brought their meal and they passed the evening with lighter conversation. After the meal, between dessert and coffee, Mackenzie stood and reached out her hand to Mick. The band was playing *Cheek to Cheek.*

"Dance with me," she commanded.

Mick's mouth twisted into a wry grin. "What will your dad's parishioners say?"

"Let them talk," Mackenzie laughed.

It was almost 11 when Mick dropped her off, and close to midnight as he fell into bed, emotionally exhausted by the events of the day. He was startled awake by the ringing of his phone. The clock read almost eight. He had overslept. He grabbed the phone and sat up. "Hello?"

"Hi Mick."

"Morgan? Are you OK?"

A childish giggle sounded from the other end of the line. "Mommy said to call. She said you would over sleep."

Mick grinned. "Your mommy is a smart lady."

"Bye, Mick. See you soon."

Before Mick could say another word, the child ended the call.

Mick crawled out of bed, showered and shaved, and let his thoughts drift to the Christmas season; pleasant thoughts of orange spiced tea, gingerbread, and pumpkin pie; of friends, family and goodwill toward men. He loved those things, and for the first time in a long time was in a place where he wanted to share those things with a special someone…with a number of special someones.

He realized he was becoming something of a homebody,

preferring the company of his fireplace and a book to the board-room; but duty called. He was due in New York for important company business this evening. He shoved a few toiletries into his overnight bag, dressed and headed for the Winston Airport, where he'd catch a puddle-jumper to Denver. From there the corporate jet would take him to the Big Apple.

He missed Mackenzie and Morgan already.

CHAPTER 43

From where Mackenzie sat, she could see the snow falling onto the playground, the wind whipping the flakes into cotton candy swirls past the window. There was an easy familiarity about the room. She had known it since she was ten years old when the church was first dedicated. The room didn't feel quite so friendly now.

She sat next to her mother around the long rectangular table. They sipped coffee from Styrofoam cups as her father, the pastor, and the six elders filed in and took their places.

"Brother Eric, would you lead us in prayer," John Austen asked, opening the meeting.

Eric George was the eldest of the elders and typically the most outspoken. There was no doubt in John's mind that the gossip and complaints swirling around his daughter were initiated by this man and his family. Still, he afforded the elder the respect due his position.

George gave the opening prayer; a formal matter replete with many 'thees' and 'thous' and concluded with a hearty 'amen and amen!' then turned his attention back to the pastor.

"I want to thank you all again for allowing Darla and Mackenzie to attend this meeting. In light of recent allegations, I thought Mackenzie should speak for herself. We, of course, will take up the church business immediately following. So, without any objections…" He nodded to Mackenzie.

Mackenzie sipped her coffee and turned her head toward her father. "Thank you, Dad." She looked at the men around the table; men she had known and respected for most of her life. *God, please give me the right words*, she prayed. She forced a smile.

"As you all no doubt know, there have been a number of insinuations, allegations, and quite frankly some outright lies made about me, my lifestyle and my career. I am here this morning to address those things." She pushed the empty cup away and clasped her hands on top of the table in front of her. "First, some people have complained about my choice of material. Honestly, I'm a little bemused by this allegation, since my CD's haven't even been released yet, and I'm pretty sure nobody in this church knows what songs will be on them. Both of my radio singles are strongly faith-centered, and I've been blessed to have cross-over success in both contemporary Christian and pop radio formats."

"Perhaps one of you saw me in concert and had a problem with one of the songs I performed?" She looked around the room. No one nodded. "No? Gentlemen, I've been singing since before I can remember. I have always used my voice for God. Anyone who knows me knows that God's praise is continually on my lips. And yes, I have recorded a CD of secular songs. But I am not the least bit ashamed of it. I sing all my songs for Jesus." She unclasped her hands, stood and leaned forward on the table, fixing each man present with her eyes. "Gentlemen, may I ask you, have you listened to the songs on that CD? I suspect that you know the songs well, even if you haven't heard me sing them; they are all from your generation. What do you find objectionable about such standards as 'My Foolish Heart,' 'Moonlight Serenade,' or 'Don't Dream of Anyone but Me?' Does 'Exactly Like You' or 'So Rare' somehow grieve the

Holy Spirit?"

Heat climbed into Mackenzie's voice, and she struggled to maintain her composure. She held up her hand. "Oh, I know! It's 'Dancing in the Dark.' That's the one. Dancing is a sin, right? Except for when David danced before the Ark of the Covenant, or when Miriam danced after the Israelites passed through the Red Sea. And after all, that's the second charge laid at my feet, isn't it? I was seen dancing…with a man!"

Her emotions were getting the best of her and she found it impossible to control the tears that started leaking down her cheeks. "Well, shame on me!" She collapsed back into her chair, biting her lip to keep from weeping openly.

The elders all looked at one to another. Finally, Randy Boyd, the newest member of the board of elders, spoke. "Mackenzie, I've heard the rumors, but I want you to know it didn't come from me or my family. In fact, Sherry and I drove up to Denver last month to catch your concert. It was a great show. We thoroughly enjoyed it and found nothing objectionable about it."

"It's the devil's music," Eric George interrupted. "Am I the only man here willing to stand up against this rubbish?"

Every eye in the room turned to focus on the elderly man.

"Eric," John leaned back in his chair and rubbed his eyes, "What in the name of all that is holy are you talking about?"

Eric pointed a bony finger at John and chided him. "I expected you to take her side. You're her father after all. But this rock 'n' roll music is evil I tell you. It'll lead our young people down the wrong path. Why, she already admitted dancing? What next?"

Darla leaned forward with a hint of anger in her eyes.

"Eric George! I'm surprised at you. Your mother taught me piano when I was a young girl. She loved Cole Porter! What in the world has gotten into you?"

"Mmmph!" The old man responded, "She's probably dancing with the devil himself too!"

Stunned silence filled the room. Roger Barron, of an age with Eric, broke the silence. "You can't be serious," he breathed. "Your mother was a saint. She loved God with all her heart, and you know it. I can't believe you'd say such a thing. I'm ashamed of you."

Mackenzie managed to get her emotions under control, and decided that perhaps reason might be the better part of valor.

"Mr. George," Mackenzie ventured, "You've known me since I was a child. I know you love music. You always sing so beautifully when we do the old hymns. And I know you love Country music. We can all hear it blaring from your car when you come to church on Sunday mornings. I like Country too, and I'm not putting it down, but you have to admit, some of the content in Country music is less than Christian, isn't it? Why is your music okay, but mine isn't?"

A crimson flush rose up the old man's neck and onto his cheeks. He started to sweat profusely. "Don't try to change the subject, young lady!" He stood and shook his finger at her. "If you don't change your ways you are going to Hell, and you'll be responsible for leading an entire generation to Hell with you."

John Austen slammed his palm down on the table. "That's enough!"

Eric George's mouth opened and closed several times, like a fish out of water, but no more words came out. His eyes bugged out, and he raised his hand to his forehead, then toppled over and fell to the floor.

"Merciful God," Darla cried out. "Someone call 9-1-1."

CHAPTER 44

The paramedics wheeled Eric George out of the building. The siren blared as the ambulance rushed toward Winston General Hospital. It appeared the elderly man had suffered a stroke. Everyone at the meeting was visibly shaken, but Mackenzie was taking it especially hard. Randy Boyd, now the senior elder, reached across the table and patted her hand.

"Don't you feel bad about this, Mackenzie," he encouraged her. "Eric was a sick man. I fear this has been building up for a while. We could all see it. His whole personality has been changing for a few years now. I'm just sorry he took it out on you." Randy shook his head. "You know, that wasn't like Eric. He was sick is all. All we can do is pray for him now."

"Thank you, Mr. Boyd," Mackenzie managed a weak smile. "I am upset. I admit it. But not because anything that's gone on here today. That all seems insignificant in light of what we've just experienced. I'm upset because it just brought home how short life is. Mr. George might die! Don't you see? All we have is here and now. We're not promised tomorrow. The real question is, what are we going to do with today?"

She made no attempt to control the tears that were now flowing down her cheeks. "This day is all we have gentlemen; this moment and the promise of God's word. I, for one, am not going to waste another minute. I'm going to leave this room and pick up my daughter. I am going to love her as if tomorrow will never come and if it does, praise God, I will love her better."

The elders in the room nodded silently. At last her father said, "Baby, if you want to, you can preach that this Sunday. And if you don't want to, then I think maybe I will."

Mackenzie and Darla left the elders' meeting and picked Morgan up from daycare.

"Give me a hug, baby," Mackenzie said as she scooped up the toddler and smothered her with kisses. "How 'bout lunch, Pooh? But you have to be brave first. You know the routine."

Morgan giggled. "I know. Sugar reading and 'nsulin." She threw her arms open wide and closed them around her mother's neck. "I'm this brave!"

Darla watched with mixed wonder and pride. Morgan had gained weight and was speaking so much better. She couldn't believe her granddaughter was going to be three years old. *Where does the time go*, she mused. Her thoughts turned to Mick Lambert, and she let out a sign that caused Mackenzie to raise a questioning eyebrow. Darla waved the look away as if it were nothing, but secretly, Darla hoped that Mackenzie would apply her determination to love people better toward Mick. *If only Mackenzie knew how many people were praying for that outcome.*

Mackenzie parked the big green four-wheel drive truck in the McDonald's lot.

"I like Mick's truck, Mommy. Will he be back for the program? Can we call him?"

Mackenzie smiled at her mother and answered her daughter. "Yes, he will, and yes, we'll call him tonight."

They sat in a booth and watched the mixture of snow and Christmas light reflections in the window.

"Adam will be here tomorrow, Honey," Darla reminded her, "Are you excited about that?" Morgan bit into her cheeseburger and shrugged her shoulders.

"I guess," she smiled brightly and added, "Mick will be here in two days." She held up two little fingers." Can I go play in the playland, Mommy? I'm finished." Mac nodded her approval and the little girl scurried off.

"I have never seen anything like it, Mackenzie. That girl absolutely idolizes Mick Lambert." Darla sipped her coffee and shook her head. "What are you going to do about it?"

Mackenzie changed the subject.

"That was really sad about Mr. George. Mom, do you think I'm leading kids away from God, with my music and…dancing? I was pretty angry, but I don't want to be blind to my influence on people. I mean, what if he's right? Am I being scandalous?"

Darla chuckled, "My word, Baby, your father and I used to go dancing all the time when we were young, although I must say it's been a while." Darla wrinkled her nose and then declared. "As a matter of fact, it's been far too long since your father took me dancing. The next time you and Mick go to Romano's, you let me know. I'll drag your father along and we'll give those busybodies at church something to talk about."

"Thanks, Mom," Mackenzie smiled. She scanned the play area to make sure Morgan was okay, watched her wallowing in the sea of soft plastic balls, then turned back to her mother. "But what about the whole 'avoiding the appearance of evil' thing? Shouldn't I be concerned about that. I mean, I'm starting to have a pretty high profile. I really don't want to inadvertently lead someone astray."

Darla reached out and pushed a stray curl behind Mackenzie's ear. "The fact that you're asking the question means you're probably okay," she said. "Of course you don't want to give people the wrong impression. But the Word says, 'To the pure all things are pure, and to the impure nothing is pure.' People are going to see what they want to see, regardless of your motive. Follow your heart, Mackenzie, and listen to that still small voice." Darla smiled warmly at her daughter. "Are you about ready to go?"

Mackenzie returned the smile, and this time it reached her eyes. She felt lighter than she had in days. "Thanks Mom. I needed that." She nodded toward Morgan, who was squealing at the top of her lungs as she climbed through the bright red plastic tunnel. "Now I think it's time to take Mr. Lambert's Number 1 fan home for a nap."

"Oh. So, *Morgan* is Mick's Number 1 fan," Darla smirked. "Where does that leave you?"

Mackenzie put her hands on her hips. "Mom, please, don't start."

Darla raised an eyebrow. "It's not my place to start," she said. "But I think it's high time *you* started. Don't you?"

The fire crackled in the fireplace and the Christmas tree lights illuminated the Austen's living room with a warm glow. Mackenzie was settled in the corner of the sofa with her feet tucked under her, sipping hot cocoa from an oversized mug. Morgan skipped into the room, freshly bathed by her grandmother, and decked out in a festive red and green footed pajama set. She wriggled up beside her mother and reached for the cocoa.

Mackenzie gave her daughter a sip, then set the mug on a

coaster and engaged in an impromptu tickle-fight. Morgan squealed with delight and they both collapsed onto the floor in a fit of giggles and snorts.

Morgan snuggled close then whispered into her mother's ear, "Is it time to call Mick?"

Mackenzie squeezed her daughter. "It's time. Go get mommy's cell phone."

Morgan shrieked in delight. She rummaged through Mackenzie's purse until she found the device and carried it to her mother.

"Do you know the words to your song," Mackenzie asked as she regained her place on the sofa. "Can you sing it to Mick?" Morgan grinned and nodded, and climbed into Mackenzie's lap. Morgan had been watching television when someone on the show began to sing 'Pretty Baby.' She fell in love with the song and Mackenzie taught her the lyrics. Most kids her age sing '*Twinkle, Twinkle.*' My kid sings '*Pretty Baby*' and '*I've Got a Crush on You,*' Mackenzie mused.

Mackenzie started to dial Mick's number, when her cell phone rang. She couldn't prevent the smile from spreading across her face when caller ID revealed the identity of the caller.

"Hello," she said leaning back against the cushion.

"Ahh, my favorite person in the whole world. But don't tell my second favorite person," came the deep male voice.

"Mick!" She pulled her legs up under her and beamed. "It'll be our little secret. So, I was reaching for the phone when you called. I thought I was supposed to call you."

"Yes, well, let's just say I'm impatient. I miss you, Mac." He envisioned her head cocked to the side, and her fetching smile.

"Hang on. Someone wants to talk to you."

She put the cell on speaker, and Morgan launched into her rendition of 'Pretty Baby.' Mick's heart melted.

"That was amazing, Morgan," he gushed. "I can't wait to see you when I get back."

"Can't wait to see you too, Mick," the toddler replied. "Two days, 'member?"

"You've got it, baby," he said. "Let me talk to your mommy now."

Morgan nodded and trotted into the kitchen where Darla was decorating Christmas cookies, and Mackenzie took the cell phone off speaker and walked into her bedroom for a bit of privacy.

They made small talk. Mackenzie shared the momentous events of the day, and he related the boring details of his corporate responsibilities.

Mick ended by saying, "I love you."

Mackenzie ended by saying, "I'll see you soon."

He hung up the phone and wiped his eyes. *Please God,* he prayed. *I know love is supposed to be patient, but I don't know how much longer I can take it. Please help Mackenzie resolve this hurdle.*

It's gonna be another long, cold lonely night, he thought. *It's funny; I can buy just about anything a man could want. But the only thing I really want, money can't buy. Now that's what you call ironic.*

Chapter 45

Mackenzie placed her Bible on the nightstand and switched off the light. She rolled onto her stomach, closed her eyes and reflected on the events of the day. It had been a hard day, a stressful day, but in the end, a good day. She thanked God for it, and fell asleep.

When she opened her eyes, she was on stage, standing in front of a full orchestra, the players decked out in formal attire. She felt the familiar thrill as the music washed over her. She closed her eyes, tilted her head back, lifted her face toward heaven and raised the microphone to her lips. She sang. And it was beautiful!

She awoke with a start, disoriented in the total darkness of her room. She felt cold. *Was it the dream, or is my blood sugar going haywire?* She fumbled for the light, and pushed the power button on her cell phone. 2 a.m. She threw back the covers, slipped her feet into her fuzzy slippers and grabbed her robe. Picking up her glucometer, she headed to the kitchen and did a quick test.

The results are fine, she mused. *If my blood sugar is okay, why did I feel like that? Maybe a cup of hot spice tea will help.*

She put the kettle on and settled into the sofa, staring at the dying embers in the fireplace while she waited for the water to boil.

She could have simply popped a mug of water into the

microwave, but she enjoyed the ritual of making tea the old-fashioned way. She found it soothing.

Strange dream, she pondered. Usually if she had an odd or disturbing dream, the details left her as soon as she awakened, even if the feeling remained. But this dream was different. It wasn't a bad dream, or even a disturbing dream. It felt more... profound, was the only word she could match to the feeling it gave her. And she could remember every last detail.

The kettle whistled softly, and she removed it from the heat. She didn't want to disturb anyone else. She sipped the hot tea, and prayed, but found no insight into the nature of the dream. Still the tea helped relax her mind, and the lateness of the hour compelled her to return to bed.

She didn't remember closing her eyes, but the same dream reasserted itself, and she jerked back to wakefulness at 5 a.m. She fell back onto her pillow and moaned. *No sense trying to get back to sleep,* she reasoned to herself. *God must be trying to tell me something, but I have no idea what.*

She once again donned her robe and slippers and padded into the kitchen, where she discovered her mother was already awake and had coffee made.

"Trouble sleeping?" Mackenzie inquired as she poured herself a cup of coffee.

Darla nodded. "I just have this feeling of...I don't know. Something," she replied. "I can't really explain it. It's not bad. It's more like...something important is about to happen. You know what I mean?"

Mackenzie nodded back. She knew exactly what her mother meant. They sipped their coffee together in comfortable silence. Sometimes there was no need for words. They just enjoyed each other's company while they pondered their own thoughts.

At last Mackenzie excused herself. She wanted to shower before Morgan woke up. She returned a while later, her still damp hair wrapped in a towel, to find her mother with tears in her eyes.

"Mom, what's wrong," she asked.

"Eric George," Darla answered. "He didn't make it through the night. We got the call a few minutes ago. Your father has already left for the hospital."

Mackenzie's eyes widened as she thought of yesterday's altercation with the elder. She harbored no ill will toward the man, and she certainly didn't wish him dead. She was reminded once more of the shortness of life, and resolved to live as though there were no tomorrow.

"I'm so sorry," she said at last. "Did Dad say when he might be back?"

"No. You never know in these situations how long it will take. I know they had their differences, but your father needs to be there for Eric's family. He had great respect for the man Eric used to be." Darla pushed the scrambled eggs around the plate with her fork. She had lost her appetite. She turned her attention back to her daughter. "Are you OK?"

"Yes. No. I don't know," she answered. "I had a dream last that that has stayed with me. I had it twice, in fact." She shared the details of the dream with her mother; details that were just as crisp as if they had really happened. "I've never had God speak to me in a dream before, and I know it sounds like something straight out of the first century, but I can't shake the feeling that that's really what is going on. I just don't know what it is He's trying to say."

"Sometimes all we can do is pray and keep on walking," Darla said. "God is faithful. He won't leave you in the dark." Darla patted her daughter's hand, and together they cleaned breakfast dishes. Darla excused herself and left to shower and dress for the day.

Mackenzie woke Morgan and helped her pick out an outfit for the day. Morgan stood on her bed, tilted her face skyward, raised her hand and started singing at the top of her lungs. Suddenly she stopped and gazed at Mackenzie.

"Do you feel bad, Mommy?"

"No, Baby. I'm fine," Mackenzie said. "Why do you ask?"

"You're not singing with me." Her voice was tinged with disappointment.

Mackenzie shook her head and gave Morgan a big hug. "Mommy doesn't feel bad, Baby," she explained. "I just have a lot on my mind right now."

Morgan nodded her head, her red curls bouncing up and down. "It's okay, Mommy. Mick will be back tomorrow. He promised."

Maybe she knows me better than I know myself, Mackenzie thought. The truth was, she did miss that blue-eyed business magnate, more than she wanted to admit. "What song do you want to sing?" Mac asked, and was surprised when the answer was, *You've Got It, Baby!*

John Austen walked through the front door as they reached the finale. He followed the sound of their voices to Morgan's room, watched the mother/daughter duo singing their hearts out, then gave them a big hand.

Morgan curtsied and Mackenzie grinned broadly.

"There's fresh coffee in the pot. Mom is in the shower. She told me about Mr. George. I'm so sorry."

"Eric lived a long and full life," John sighed. "For most of it he was a prince of a fellow. Theda said the last few years he was battling with dementia. It changed him. The stroke was more than his body could handle."

"Are you hungry, Dad? Did you eat before you left? I can whip you up some breakfast." Mackenzie stood and headed toward the kitchen followed by her father.

"I grabbed a bite on the way home, but that coffee smells good." He sat at the table while Mackenzie fixed breakfast for Morgan. She poured two steaming cups of coffee for the adults. She placed one in front of her father, then sat down next to him.

"Daddy…"

"Daddy? Uh oh. What's the problem?" He peered at her over the top of his glasses.

"Why, whatever do you mean," she asked feigning astonishment.

"Come on, Baby. Anytime you start the conversation with, 'Daddy,' it always means trouble." Spit it out. I know money's not an issue anymore, and you certainly don't need to borrow the car, so what's up?" He smiled at her. "Come on. Tell daddy all about it."

Mackenzie laughed. "Busted," she admitted. "Alright… *Daddy.*"

Mackenzie shared her dream, just as she had with her mother. She couldn't shake the feeling that it was important, and she didn't want to miss out on whatever it meant.

Her father closed his eyes and smiled. "Well, I'm no Joseph or Daniel, and I've never claimed to be an interpreter of dreams, but I think it might have something to do with your Mr. Lambert."

"Mick? Why? He wasn't even in my dream," she sputtered.

"Perhaps not in the flesh, so to speak," John explained. "But think back. In your dream, what song were you singing?"

"'Secret Love,'" she said.

John nodded. "And who originally recorded the song?"

"Doris Day," Mackenzie answered immediately. "You know that as well as I do. It's from the movie, 'Calamity Jane'. We own the DVD. But what does that have to do with Mick?"

John nodded again. "As I recall, she sang that song when she realized who it was she was in love with."

The shock of realization washed over Mackenzie's face.

"Dad, you know…"

"Oh, now it's 'Dad' now, huh?" John laughed.

"It's not funny, Dad," Mackenzie fumed. "I know it in my head, but I just can't say it in my heart." Fat tears welled up in her eyes and overflowed down her cheeks. "I told Mick that when I was able to say the words, I would tell him I love him. But I can't say it. I… can't… say … it!"

Mackenzie covered her face in her hands and started weeping, her body shuddering from heart-wrenching sobs.

John put his arm around her and pulled her to his chest. Morgan stared at her mother, unable to comprehend the emotions that had overcome her. Her lower lip quivered, and she began to cry as well.

Darla heard the commotion and rushed into the kitchen. "What's going on," she demanded. "What's wrong?"

John patted his daughter's back with one hand and with the other motioned for Darla to tend to Morgan. "We're okay, sweetheart," he told her. "Mackenzie's just had a rough couple of days. I think she just got hit with a bit of revelation."

Darla gathered Morgan into her arms and soothed the crying child. "You're okay," she whispered. "You're okay, and your Mommy's okay. Say, how's about you come with Grandma and we'll go to the airport to pick up Aunt Wendy. Won't that be fun?"

Morgan gave a final shuddering sniff and nodded.

"Thanks Mom," Mackenzie managed between sobs. "I'll be okay. But I'm going to look a mess when Wendy gets here."

"We'll be back soon." Darla smiled and patted her daughter's back. She didn't want to leave, but she knew her husband would handle the crisis while she was away. She grabbed her purse and walked out the door.

John gave Mackenzie time to compose her emotions, then he handed her a box of tissues. "Now, tell me why you can't say I love you to the man you obviously *do* love."

Mackenzie sniffed softly. "I told a man I loved him once, and you saw how that ended. I was... *an inconvenience...* to him." She looked into her father's eyes. "He never even saw his own daughter. The only thing that mattered to him was money and prestige."

"Honey, I'm pretty sure the last thing Mick Lambert needs is money or prestige."

"No," Mackenzie countered. "He doesn't need money, or prestige. He's everything that Jared wasn't. He's rich, and he's handsome, and he's charming, and...and..." her voice trailed off to a breathless whisper. "And I'm nothing. I'm just a single mom from the middle of nowhere. What if he gets tired of me?"

"I realize there are plenty of men who use women for their own vanity. But not all men do. I'm a man. I've been faithful to your mother for more than thirty years. She is the light of my life. Think about the things he has done for you and Morgan. What does he have to gain from it? He either loves you with every fiber of his being, or he's a complete nutcase." John paused for a moment and smiled. "Mick Lambert doesn't strike me as being a nutcase."

He rose and refreshed their coffee cups.

"Not much worse than cold coffee to go along with a good cry," he quipped, which brought a quick chuckle from Mackenzie.

He regained his seat next to his daughter and continued. "I can't tell you to trust Mick. But as your earthly father, I can tell you to trust your heavenly Father. Look, Mackenzie; I know you are afraid. God knows you have a right to be. But sometimes you have to take a step of faith."

Mackenzie hugged her father's neck. "Thanks, Daddy," she said. "That helps a lot. I still don't know that I'm ready to say those words, but you certainly helped me put some things in perspective."

CHAPTER 46

Darla sat down on the couch by Wendy. A fire blazed in the fireplace casting a warm glow across the living room. In the corner, Christmas tree lights twinkled and reflected off the tinsel. Morgan lay on the floor, coloring happily in the activity book her Aunt Wendy had brought from Dallas. Mackenzie lay next to her, head propped on a pillow, enjoying the nearness of her precocious child.

"Aren't you two uncomfortable down there?" Wendy asked.

"Oh no," Mackenzie replied, "The carpet is cozy."

"What I want to know is, where are the men?" Darla chimed in.

Wendy laughed, "They're out in the garage, drooling over little sister's new toy."

Morgan cut in. "It's not her toy, it's a Corvette. Mommy's toy is her microphone, isn't that right Mommy," the child looked up at her mother expectantly.

"That's right, baby," Mackenzie giggled.

Wendy shook her head. "Must be nice to be able to pay cash for a thing like that. Makes me wish I could sing. Why don't you drive it?"

"You've obviously never tried to drive a sports car in the snow and ice," Mackenzie quipped.

"Not really," Wendy replied. "We don't get a lot of snow and ice in Dallas, and sports cars aren't high on the list of affordable cars when you're on a teacher's salary."

Wendy grew pensive and shook her head. "Sis, Mom said you had a real insight the other day at church. Anything you can share?"

"I guess, it just hit me about how brief our time on earth really is. We need to gather rosebuds while we may. You and Bryan need to spend as much time with Adam as you can. He'll be grown before you know it. Dad showed me an old photo of me this morning. Thinking back on it, it seems as though it were only yesterday."

"Truth," Darla said. "Kids grow up before you know it."

"We try as much as possible, but life gets in the way," Wendy countered. "You above everyone know how hectic teaching can be, Mom. Bryan and I are fortunate in that we have student assistants to handle some of the load. We like it though. I can't see us doing anything else. And trust me, Adam gets plenty of attention; don't let him tell you different." She tucked her legs beneath her and shifted to a different subject. "What was it about that dream you had that had you so upset?"

Mackenzie sighed audibly. *Does everybody in the family know my business?* She looked at her mother and then sister and began to sing, "…I had the craziest dream last night." She broke off the song and said, "It wasn't the dream itself as much as it was that it just kept recurring, every time I closed my eyes."

"Sounds like this is going to be a long story," Darla interrupted. "Who wants hot chocolate?" They all went to the kitchen where Darla made a pot of the rich, hot liquid.

Wendy wandered down the hall to the garage entrance and looked outside.

"The men aren't out there," Wendy announced, "And Dad's car is gone."

"That's odd. Your father rarely leaves without letting me know where he's going and when he'll be back," Darla mused.

"Hey, Mackenzie, does Mick still have that, uh, what do you call it," Wendy asked.

"You mean the beast?" Darla quipped.

"Yes, and her name is Gringolet," Mackenzie smiled.

"Mick's toy!" Morgan shouted from the living room where she was still happily coloring outside the lines.

"Has she ridden in it," Wendy asked.

"Oh, yes. Tell them about it, Morgan." Mackenzie prompted.

"Gringlay makes lots of noise and it blows my hair and it's really fast," the toddler smiled. "It's Mick's toy."

"I see. So, Morgan you really like Mick a lot, huh," Wendy asked.

Morgan shook her head seriously. "No, I don't like him," she said making a face, "I love him!"

Mackenzie choked on the cocoa she was sipping.

"Yes, well…," Darla fumbled, looking at Mackenzie.

Wendy just smiled and sipped her coca. "So, Baby, when did you decide you love Mick?"

Morgan shrugged her shoulders.

"Let's see," Wendy directed her questions toward Mackenzie, "I remember the day we met in Pediatrics. Could it have been the day he became the Legend of the Ward?"

Mackenzie sat trance-like, staring at her daughter.

"Uh, earth to sister, hello? Hello? Anybody in there?" Wendy waved her hand in front of Mackenzie's face.

Mackenzie slowly mouthed something under her breath. "Yes! Yes! Yes!" She shouted at the top of her lungs. She jumped up, picked up Morgan, and placed her in a tight hug. They danced around the kitchen. Morgan seemed to be having a great time. Darla and Wendy did not know what to think. After several minutes, Mackenzie sat down with her daughter in her lap who was giggling and enjoying herself.

"Honey, are you all right," Darla asked.

"Mother," Mackenzie glowed, a rosy blush flushing her cheeks. "I am better than I have ever been!"

CHAPTER 47

The wind spit mingled snow and sleet into the two men's faces as they walked toward the shopping mall. The warmth just inside the entrance stood in stark contrast to the sub-freezing temperatures outside. They brushed the snow from their shoulders and stomped the icy residue from their feet.

"Gordon, you really should start your Christmas shopping earlier. Look at the crowd! We'll be lucky if all the good gifts haven't already been picked over," Mick teased his good friend Gordon Palmer. "Do you have any idea what Beth would like?"

"Only everything, my friend," Gordon replied. "Only everything."

The mall was festooned with gaudy decorations, and Christmas music wafted throughout the common area in a joyful cacophony of sound. A familiar voice permeated the music, bringing a lump to Mick's throat.

I might not be with Mackenzie right now, he thought, *but I'm surrounded by her just the same.* Not only were multiple stores playing her hit songs; he even saw a life-size cardboard cutout in the display window of a music store. Her picture was on magazine covers at the news stand, and a teen apparel shop featured a rack of T-shirts with her face boldly emblazoned on the front.

Gordon put his hand on Mick's shoulder. "The lady seems to be everywhere."

Everywhere except in my home, as my wife, Mick thought. "So, Gordon, how about a bit of nice jewelry for Beth? You know how women love sparkly baubles."

"Beth loves diamonds, but my bank account doesn't," Gordon protested as they entered the jewelry store.

"Come on, Gordon. I have it on good authority that you just received a nice Christmas bonus. Come on, Scrooge. Open up that wallet and make your lady happy," Mick laughed.

Gordon chose an elegant pearl necklace and a pair of diamond earrings. While the clerk gift-wrapped his purchase he observed his young friend, who was leaning on a display case of engagement rings.

Mick caught the expression on Gordon's face. "I thought you had already bought Mackenzie a Christmas present, so I assume this is something…extra?"

"Maybe," Mick grinned. The clerk placed a lovely, one-carat, emerald-cut diamond solitaire in front of them. "What do you think, Gordon? Not too flashy, is it?"

"No, not too flashy," the older man replied. "So, you're sure? She's the one? You are going to propose?"

"The thought has crossed my mind, Gordon." Mick nodded to the clerk and handed her his credit card. "I'll take it."

They walked to the food court for a coffee while the ring was being sized. Mick stared into the steaming black liquid, and made a confession to his friend. "I don't mind telling you, Gordon, I'm terrified."

Gordon studied Mick for a moment, blew across his coffee and took a sip. "Of what?"

"You and Beth have been married how long now; forty-three years? When you popped the question, did it ever occur to you that she might say, *No?* I dunno, maybe you weren't scared.

But Mackenzie has had some demons from her past she's been wrestling with. I love her with my whole heart, and I'm pretty sure she loves me too, but I don't know if she's ready to make that commitment, and I don't want to push too hard, but I'm afraid if I don't ask her I'll miss the opportunity…and I'm really starting to babble, aren't I?"

The older man shook his head and chuckled. "When it comes to women, no man is ever 100 percent sure of what her reaction will be in any situation, particularly when it comes to a proposal. The best you can do is gird up your loins and go into battle with a stout heart. If she says, *Yes*, can I be your best man?"

Mick laughed lightly. "You've got it, baby."

They killed a bit more time, and when they stopped back at the jewelry store the ring was waiting for them.

"Thank you for your purchase, Mr. Lambert. I'm sure the lady will be pleased with your choice." The clerk placed the ring box in a bag and handed it to him.

I hope you're right, Mick thought as they left the shop.

Chapter 48

"Hello, Mick." Mackenzie's voice was joyful and more exuberant than he remembered in a long time. "How are you? How's New York? Are you ready to come home?"

"Of course, I'm ready to come home," Mick laughed. "I think Beth and Gordon are ready for me to 'come home' too." Hearing her voice just made him miss her all the more.

Mackenzie's voice took on a coquettish tone. "You'll be home in time for the Christmas pageant at church tomorrow night, right? It's really important that you be there, because, well, I got permission from Dad and, uh… Morgan and I are doing a special for you. It's a Christmas present from us!"

"I don't understand. What's a *special*?"

"You know. A *special*. Morgan and I are going to sing a special song… just for you. I already made all the arrangements. Rob is going to pick you up at the airport and bring you to the church. Patty is saving a place for you." She lowered her voice into a husky whisper. "Don't be late, Mr. Lambert. If you are, you will have two very disappointed, broken-hearted redheads on your hands. You don't want that, do you?"

Mick swallowed hard. "No, ma'am. That would be the last thing I want. I will be there."

"I'll see you tomorrow night, then," Mackenzie breathed. "Good night Mick."

Mick disconnected the call just as Beth called from the

kitchen, "Fresh coffee, Mick." Mick padded into the kitchen in his stocking feet as Beth poured the coffee and sat down beside Gordon.

"Gordon tells me you're thinking seriously about taking the plunge. Tell me about this girl who has stolen your heart. What's she like? And what would your marriage be like to her? I understand she is a singer who is on the road a lot. And she has a little girl? Who looks after her when her mother is gone? Would you get to see your wife very often?"

Mick grinned at her. This woman he had known all his life, was asking all the questions a mother would ask. Since his mother had long since passed, he supposed Beth had assumed that mantle.

"You know, Beth, it's not like I keep office hours. When she goes on the road, there's no reason I can't go with her. But let's not jump the gun just yet. I haven't asked her to marry me yet, and she hasn't said, *Yes*. Why do I get the impression that you aren't in favor of this marriage?"

"Mick, it's not that I'm opposed to you getting married, but this girl is a single mother, from a backwater community in the middle of fly-over country. You have such a tender heart, and I don't know what this girl's motives are. I hope at least you will have her sign a prenuptial agreement. Gordon and I think that would be advisable."

Mick was dumbfounded. "A pre-nup? Gordon, just this afternoon you said you wanted to be my best man!"

"Take it easy Mick," Gordon pleaded. "We're only thinking of your best interests. That's my job – as your friend and as an officer with Lambert Group."

"Gordon, you've known me my whole life. I'm the last person to rush into a relationship. And Beth, if Gordon asked you to sign a pre-nup before he proposed to you, would you have said Yes? I'm sorry, but going into a marriage worried about how it's going to turn out seems like a poor way to start. Look, I appreciate your concern, both of you, but this is my life. And honestly, the Lambert Group doesn't have any say in it."

"I'm sorry, Mick," Beth shook her head. "It's just that so much has changed in society since we got married. I meant no offense."

"I know you didn't," Mick managed a weak smile. "I didn't mean to get angry. But she is the woman I love after all. And Gordon, if Mackenzie does accept to my proposal, I certainly hope you would consider standing with me, as my Best Man."

He kissed Beth on the cheek, then headed back toward the guest room. Slipping between the sheets, he turned off the light and closed his eyes. In his heart, he knew he was right about Mackenzie. There was no way she was after him for his money. But sleep was still a long time coming.

CHAPTER 49

Morgan and Jamie sat on the floor captivated by the antics of the morning children's show. Their mothers relaxed and engaged in conversation on the overstuffed sofa in Patty's living room. Heavy snow continued to fall outside the picture window.

"I hope this storm doesn't cause any trouble at the airport. It would be too bad if Mick's plane was delayed." Patty held her hot chocolate in both hands. She looked quizzically at her friend. "Okay, out with it. I can tell when you're hiding something. We're best friends. Why all the secrecy?"

Mackenzie smiled at her best friend. "Because if I told you it wouldn't be a surprise." Mackenzie sipped her own hot chocolate and pushed back into the cushions. "You will just have to wait and see, like everybody else."

Mackenzie placed her empty cup on the coffee table, glanced at the children to make sure they were occupied, then leaned close to Patty. "I know, deep down in my heart, that I love Mick Lambert," she confessed. "The problem is, I'm scared. I am scared to tell him."

Patty pulled back and looked into Mackenzie's eyes.

"Alright, girlfriend, we've skirted this issue ever since we've known each other. Let's get down to business. Exactly what makes it so hard for you to tell the man you love him?"

"Jared Costino," Mackenzie whispered.

"Jared?" Patty sputtered. "I don't mean to speak ill of the

dead, but Jared was a Grade-A heel. He was arrogant, pompous, money-hungry and full of himself. Talk about the complete opposite of Mick Lambert. Why would you let the memory of a jerk like Jared keep you from declaring your love for, dare I say it, God's gift to women?"

"Well, when you put it like that," Mackenzie giggled and held up her hands. "Seriously, Patty, it's not that simple. I know Mick isn't Jared. On his worst day, Mick is a million time better than my ex." She paused and thought for a moment. "Ex. Is that an appropriate term when he's deceased? Technically, I'm a widow, so... I don't know, but you know what I mean."

She pulled her knees up to her chin and wrapped her arms around them. "After the events of the past few days, including my weird dreams, I really feel like I've had a revelation from God. It's like God is telling me that it's okay for me to be in love with Mick."

"So what's the hold up?" Patty demanded. "You've got the OK from the Big Guy Himself."

"It's not that easy," Mackenzie countered.

"How does he love you; let me count the ways," Patty interrupted. She held up one hand and started counting on her fingers. "One; he brought Rob to hear you sing, which launched your career as a recording artist. Two; he got your baby in to see you when you were in the hospital. Three; your tycoon friend is handling your investments, making you into an independently wealthy woman. Four; he introduced Rob to me. Okay, that's more about me than you, but I gotta love him for that."

Both women giggled like schoolgirls for a moment. Then Patty grew serious. "Mackenzie, the man is on your side! A blind man could see it. He's head over heels for you. And on top of everything else, he loves your daughter." Patty leaned back and sighed heavily. "Of course I haven't mentioned that he's rich, attractive, Christian and, oh yeah, if you happen to need a company rep for the diabetic pumps, I'm pretty sure *he knows a guy*. After all, he owns the company."

Mackenzie stuck out her tongue, then a smile graced her lips. "Thank you, Patty. That helped a lot. Now, for something really important. "Do you want to help me with the plan?"

CHAPTER 50

Wendy Collins placed another log on the fire and settled onto the couch beside her sister. "I hope your boyfriend isn't delayed by the storm."

"I'm sure he'll be on time," Darla Austen said. "I think it will take more than snow to keep him away."

Mackenzie paced nervously, constantly checking the app on her phone for updates on flights from New York. "I'm sorry. I'm nervous as a cat on a hot tin roof about tonight. I've just worked so hard to plan this, and now if Mick doesn't make it back... I'm sorry. Guess I should have more faith, huh?"

Morgan came running into the room, fat tears streaming down her face and her cousin Adam following tentatively behind.

"Mommy, Adam said I don't sing good," Morgan wailed.

Wendy gave an exasperated sigh. "Adam! Have you been tormenting your cousin? You apologize to Morgan right now, young man."

The little boy shuffled his feet and muttered, "Sorry."

Morgan clung to her mother and glowered at Adam. Mackenzie hugged Morgan and told her, "Listen baby, you could be the best singer ever and some people won't like you. Don't let that bother you, okay? You just sing because you want to; because you love it. If you love it, then you keep at it. You just do it. It doesn't matter what anyone says."

She kissed Morgan on the top of her head. Her voice took

on a playful tone. "How brave are you? This much?" She held up her left hand index finger and thumb barely apart. "I need you to help me sing for Mick tonight, you going to help me?"

The little girl giggled, nodded her head and spread her arms wide. "I'm *this* brave!" she declared.

CHAPTER 51

When Mick woke from his nap, the company jet was four hundred miles from Winston. He had a ring in his pocket, a question he was ready to ask, and no idea if the woman he was going to ask that question to was ready to say 'Yes.'

Okay, admit it, he thought, *you are terrified.* He leaned back in his seat and gazed out the window. The sun was painting the clouds a coral pink, and the sky on the horizon was streaked with blue-gray. *Beautiful,* he thought. *Strange how all the colors in nature blend perfectly. None of the colors clash. Only God can make a sunset.*

His thoughts turned back to Mackenzie; to how her emerald eyes complemented her lovely red hair, which perfectly accentuated her smiling face. *She is so beautiful, like sunset on steroids,* he smiled.

Ordinarily Mick would have flown into Denver and caught a commuter plane to Winston. Tonight was too important to risk a snow delay at Denver International. He directed the pilot to fly direct to Winston Metro Airport. The Gulfstream G6500 landed amid light snow flurries, and Mick stepped off the jet into a winter wonderland.

Yeah, he thought. *Now this looks like home.*

Rob met him at the gate and pulled him into a big bear hug. "Hey Mick! It's about time you got back. I was beginning to think you were going to stay in New York."

"Are you kidding? I couldn't get back fast enough. Just the thought of living in the big city again is enough to give me the shakes. I'll take a Rocky Mountain sunset over a Manhattan skyline any day."

Mick tossed his luggage into the trunk of Rob's car, then hopped into the passenger seat and fastened his safety belt and Rob eased into the traffic. They drove in silence for several moments before Mick said, "So, what's this big surprise that Mackenzie has in store?"

"Seriously? Brother, Patty would skin me alive if I revealed the details of the evening." Rob chuckled. "Take my advice and just relax and enjoy the show. Trust me; your lady friend and her daughter have gone to a lot of trouble just for you."

He turned his head toward his friend and grinned. "Oh, by the way. Remember that interview Mackenzie did in Dallas, where she was asked who *You've Got It, Baby!* was written for?"

Mick nodded, "Yeah, I remember. Why?"

"No reason," Rob laughed. "It just came to mind."

Rob turned into the parking lot of Winston Faith Center. The lot was packed, forcing him to park on the outskirts.

"Stay with me. Patty is holding us places. Do not, I repeat do not charge the stage when you see her." Rob punched Mick on the arm and laughed.

Mick joined in the laughter, but he could feel his heart rate increase. He had only been gone two days, but his decision to buy a ring heightened his anticipation of seeing her again. He wasn't sure he could keep from rushing to her once he actually laid eyes on Mackenzie again.

The sanctuary was filled nearly to capacity by the time they entered. Mick was glad Patty arrived early and saved seats for them. They had a great view of the platform from their seats in the center section, midway down.

"Hello, Mick," she whispered, giving him a light hug.

"Hey, yourself," Mick retorted. "I leave town a few days and you guys cook up a suspense story for me? What's up with that?"

John Austen strode to the podium. "Shh," Patty pushed a finger to her lips. "Quiet! Trust me you'll like it."

"Good evening!" John intoned. "Welcome to our Christmas pageant. We hope you'll join in as we celebrate the true meaning of Christmas." John prayed, then turned the stage over to the children's choir. A little boy dressed as a shepherd, and looking very much like Linus in the Peanuts Christmas special, recited the story of Jesus birth. Then children sang, resulting in thunderous applause and beaming faces from proud parents and grandparents. The adult choir followed, and accompanied by a 20-piece orchestra, enthralled the audience with a magnificent collection of classic Christmas songs, as well as favorite contemporary pieces that celebrated the birth of Christ. It was a moving and worshipful event.

The choir left the stage, John once more took up the microphone. "It's been a wonderful evening of worship and adoration for our Lord. But before we close, we have one more very special song for you from our own Mackenzie Austen."

The crowd erupted in applause, cheers and whistles as Mackenzie mounted the platform and took the microphone from her father.

"Good evening everyone," she smiled, "A while back I made a promise to Lynn Montgomery of *Good Morning, Dallas!* that when I was ready to reveal the inspiration behind the song, *You've Got It, Baby!* she would be the first to know. Well, Ms. Montgomery is with us tonight as our very special guest, because tonight I'm going to tell her, and you, the story behind the song."

Once again, the crowd roared its approval. Mackenzie waited with a beatific smile on her face until the crowd settled down. She scanned the crowd until her eyes found Mick's face. Her smile broadened, she pointed at him, raised the microphone to her lips and said, "The inspiration for *You've Got It, Baby!* is Michael David Lambert IV."

The crowd turned and stared in his direction, but Mick was oblivious to them all. His complete focus was on the diminutive redhead on the stage.

"You see, I met Mick in the parking lot, right out front." She giggled at the memory. "I was a damsel in distress, and like a knight in shining armor, he came swooping in to rescue me. For those of you who do not know the story, my daughter Morgan was gravely ill, and Mick, who was a complete stranger, took us to the hospital."

She stopped and smiled. "The next day, Mick came to the hospital to check on Morgan, and she just fell in love with him, and asked him if he would come back and visit the next day. He said he would, and Morgan looked up at him with those big eyes of hers and said, 'Promise?'" Mackenzie pouted her lips in her best Morgan impersonation, which drew a hearty laugh and many 'awws' from the crowd. "Mick pointed at her and said, 'You've got it, baby!' So, now you know the story behind the song."

As Mackenzie told her story, the musicians had quietly taken their places on stage. She nodded and they launched into the intro to *You've Got It, Baby!* Mackenzie pointed to Morgan and motioned for her to join her. Darla carried Morgan to the stage, and the toddler ran to her mother. One of the backup singers handed Morgan a microphone and the crowd rose to its feet.

"Ladies and Gentlemen, May I introduce to you my daughter, Morgan Austen! Morgan and I have been working on a special gift for Mr. Lambert. It's not exactly a Christmas song, but with your permission, we'd like to sing it for you."

The audience responded with explosive applause. Mackenzie looked straight at Mick.

"Mr. Lambert, Morgan and I wish you a very Merry Christmas."

Mick was sure a stupid grin was pasted onto his face, but he was powerless to change his expression. He cheered as loud as everyone else as Mackenzie and Morgan sang.

"A walk in the park... the song of the lark... You've got it, Baby!" Mackenzie sang and Morgan emulated what she had seen her mother do countless times; holding the microphone out to the crowd for a response. Halfway through the song, Mackenzie stopped singing and just started talking as the musicians continued to play.

"Mick, you remember I told you that my heart was bound up in fear, but that when I was able, I would say the words to you. Well. that day is today, because I've learned, *Perfect love casts out fear."*

There was a collective gasp, as if everyone in the auditorium held their breath as the same time.

Mackenzie broke into tears, half-speaking, half-crying, "Mick Lambert, I love you!"

Mick could no longer contain himself. He pushed his way to the aisle and rushed for the stage. Morgan put the microphone to her lips and shouted, "Mick! Me and Mommy love you, Mick! We want you to marry us, Mick!"

Mick climbed onto the platform, oblivious to the cheering crowd. He embraced his two redheads, lifted them off the floor and twirled them around. He kissed Mackenzie, and whispered a question into her ear. She smiled and nodded. Mick got down on one knee, looked Morgan in the eye and said, "You've got it, Baby!"

ABOUT THE AUTHOR

Mike Carmichael is a classic car enthusiast with a deep romantic streak who calls Louisiana home.

You've Got It, Baby! is his first novel

Also Available From

WORDCRAFTS PRESS

Maggie's Song
   by Marcia Ware

End of Summer
   by Michael Potts

A Purpsoe True
   by Gail Kittleson

Furious
   by Aaron Shaver

Home
   by Eleni McKnight

Martyr's Moon
   by J.E. Lowder

Ill Gotten Gain
   by Ralph E. Jarrells

www.wordcrafts.net

Made in the USA
San Bernardino, CA
18 October 2018